THE BOOK

OF

MEGAN

WALLACE F. BROWN

Solebury Press

SoleburyPress@comcast.net

You need to spend time crawling alone through shadows to truly appreciate what it is to stand in the Sun.

Shaun Hick

1

Most of the time we are barely present in our lives. We insulate ourselves with our schedules and routines and our self imposed obligations. We surround ourselves with people who see the world exactly as we do. As if consensus is somehow the same thing as truth. As if we even have the capacity to comprehend what existence is at all. It's how we comfort ourselves in the face of what seems a cold and indifferent universe. But sometimes life conspires to teach us something new. The wheel turns and a different window opens up before us. A new perspective on the world. For me it often happens when I'm lost in transit. Stranded in an airport somewhere or stuck on a train. When there is nothing to do but wait, and no one to talk to but strangers.

A few years ago I was on a bus traveling through upstate New York. Buffalo was getting slammed by an early Spring snowstorm and my flight from Boston had been diverted to Rochester. I hadn't been on a bus since I was in high school and never in the middle of the night. The lights were turned down low for sleeping but I was wide awake, just staring at the snow falling outside my window. The bus was eerily quiet and it felt to me as if time had been suspended. There was an older gentleman sitting next to me and after a while we struck up a conversation. We sat there in the dim light of a reading lamp speaking in hushed tones, as if something of great importance were hanging in the balance. Like spies enmeshed in some slowly unfolding, clandestine conspiracy.

He was a professor of History, but since his retirement he had been spending his time researching some of the many unexplained events he had come across during his studies. He told me he had always been a skeptic and believed there was a rational explanation for everything. Even for things that seemed to defy logic. He conceded that everyone's experience in the world is unique, but he believed it was simply a matter of perception. As he put it, 'The sky is the sky and a stone is a stone. The same for a beggar or a king on his throne'. But the more he examined these unexplained events over the years, the more he found himself considering an alternative explanation. That there are forces at the edges of our perception that can, and often do alter our experience of the world. He had begun to believe that we are all complicit in the architecture of our own individual reality. And that we conjure our own angels and demons to help or to harry us, not by some act of will, but by the fundamental power of belief and by the primal force of fear. Change what you believe, and you can change your world. I have thought about that conversation often in the years since, but I never took the idea all that seriously. Until events conspired to challenge my own beliefs, and to make me question if I really understood the world at all.

To begin with, I shouldn't have been at that rest stop on the turnpike that Tuesday afternoon. I was planning to drive straight through to Baltimore and spend the night at the Inner Harbor. I wanted to sit out on a dock a while and listen to the boats whispering to each other in the dark. I wanted to hear the buoys singing out in the channel. There was nothing of the winter in it, and I needed to start my journey with winter at my back. I knew there was a storm coming up the coast and I should have given it another day to pass, but my suitcase was staring at me from beside the door with the forlorn look of an old dog begging to go out for a walk. I couldn't stop myself from looking at it and I was tired of sleeping in an empty house. So I woke up early, threw my bag into the back of my SUV, and headed down the road beneath the still leafless trees of the Green Mountains. It was a chilly New England morning under a pinwheel of darkening clouds. Patches of dirty snow still clung to the hillsides like an unmade bed, but the smell of distant rain was heavy in the air. I thought I might feel nostalgic, leaving this place where I had spent most of my life, especially since I wasn't sure I would ever come back. For me, on that morning though, it felt like I was making my escape. New England was just starting to awaken from its long, frozen dream. The sleepy, gray landscape was just another reason not to look in the rear view mirror.

I don't know if it was the storm causing chaos farther to the south or some apocalyptic accident somewhere ahead on the highway, but as soon as I crossed the George Washington Bridge the traffic slowed to a crawl. I could feel myself growing tense and angry, but after an hour or so of clutching the steering wheel in a death grip and straining to see through the traffic, I finally just said 'the hell with it' and made myself relax. There was no schedule. No one waiting for me. No planes to catch. Almost without thinking, I took my watch off and threw it into the glove compartment. When I looked back up at the highway, I saw the exit ramp for the rest area. It felt like my car had made its own decision to pull off the highway and relax for a while. It was fine by me.

I noticed her almost as soon as I got out of the car. She was standing next to the entrance watching the people come and go and trying, I imagined, to look inconspicuous. She looked too fragile to be out on the road alone, but then most of the young people I saw out in the world looked like they should still be in a classroom somewhere, ignoring the teacher and texting each other about the truly important things. No one seemed to take much notice of her, except for a few truckers who stared long enough to earn a quick and withering glare of dismissal. To me, she stood out like a cactus flower. She was wearing a worn looking, lime green ski jacket that was a size too large and jeans with the knees torn out of them. She had a pair of tan bedroom slippers on her feet and a tattered backpack slung carelessly over one shoulder. Her hair was red, like an ember, and she wore it feathered around her face. My first thought was that she was a runaway, but then I saw her eyes. Sapphire blue and still. There was no fear there. No uncertainty. She was scanning the crowd, her glance moving from face to face. Rejecting some out of hand. Lingering a millisecond on others.

Silent judgments, absolute and indelible. Like a nightclub bouncer who had seen it all before. And then her eyes locked onto mine and something subliminal passed between us. A two minute conversation condensed into a heartbeat. I smiled at her briefly as I passed through the door and then let my attention run free again to drift as it would.

I waited for a while at the hostess stand before a middle-aged woman with a dour expression and an armful of menus collected me and ushered me to a booth by the window. She dropped one of the menus onto the table and slid it over in front of me like a dealer at a blackjack table. After mumbling something about the waitress, she turned her back and walked away without ever making eye contact. The menu was a large laminated thing with optimistic pictures of the various lunch offerings. I studied it for a moment and when I put it down on the table, the girl was sitting across from me. She wasn't smiling. She was staring into me with those eyes as if to say, 'Here I am. What are you going to do about it?' I smiled at her again, not knowing quite how to react. I was a little startled and before I could come up with a useful question, she spoke.

"I haven't had anything to eat since yesterday."

My mind stalled somewhere between wanting to know why she had settled on me and how she had ended up in whatever fix she was in, so I just turned the menu around and slid it over to her.

"Order whatever you want."

She was studying the menu when the waitress came over.

"Coffee?"

I nodded my head. "Black"

"How about you sweetie?"

The girl gave her a disapproving look. "I'll have a large Diet Coke."

She watched the waitress for a moment as she moved on to the next table, and then she removed her jacket and put it on the seat next to her. She looked out the window for a moment and then she took a deep breath and turned her attention back to me. She tilted her head a little and her eyes narrowed. There was no shyness about her. Nothing that felt like gratitude, either. I guess I expected some kind of hard luck story,

7

real or manufactured. It didn't really matter one way or the other. I was just helping someone who was hungry. I had no idea yet, that she had other plans for me. I sat there in bemused silence as she began the process of inserting herself into my life.

"So, you're somebody. Who are you?"

"My name is Mark. Who do you think I am?"

"I don't know yet, but you're somebody."

"I don't know what that means."

She shrugged her shoulders. "We'll see. Anyway, I'm Megan."

I reached my hand across the table and she held out her fist. It wasn't anything like aggression. It was more like, 'we don't know each other well enough yet to hold hands'. It was the first of what would be many clues to the puzzle that was Megan. She was a deliberate person and she didn't waste any time getting to the point. There was nothing coarse about her manner though. No street attitude.

"So you don't have to worry. I know I look young but I just turned twenty last month."

"Twenty is young."

"Not for everyone. Not for me."

I let that pass. She was wearing a white cotton sweater with the sleeves pulled up to her elbows and I glanced at her forearms. She was small-boned, almost delicate with clear, china-white skin.

"I'm not a junkie, either, if that's what you're looking for."

"No, I didn't think that. Are you running away?"

"Running away means you have someplace to run from. I'm just going somewhere else, that's all."

"Are you in some kind of trouble?"

She laughed. "Trouble? My whole life is trouble. Everyone around me is trouble, maybe even you. Are you trouble, Mark?"

"Not to you."

"But you're trouble to somebody right? Your wife, your boss, your kids. Somebody."

"At this moment, in my life, I am trouble to no one that I know of."

"So where is she? Your wife I mean."

"What makes you think I'm married?"

"It's all over you. Besides, I can still see the ghost of a ring on your finger. You used to wear a watch too. Did you divorce both of them?"

"She passed away."

She studied my face for a moment. Searching, I imagined, for some measure of the pain those words had caused me. The waitress returned with the drinks and then took our order. After she left, Megan looked at me again.

"I'm sorry. About your wife I mean. Did you love her?"

I hesitated a moment before answering, a little startled by her frankness. No one had ever asked me that question. At least not since Ann had died. I don't think I had even asked myself.

"Yes," I said finally."But we were separated when it happened."

She nodded and was quiet for a moment.

"How long ago?"

"Almost a year."

"Did you have kids?"

"No"

She put her elbows on the table and rested her chin on her hands. Her eyes were moving across my face, studying me like some newly discovered artifact. I didn't look away. Somewhere deep inside I felt like I was suddenly being called upon to defend my life. As if Megan was some kind of gatekeeper sent to decide where fate would lead me next. She had taken complete control of the conversation, almost as if she was the one doing me a favor. I was too intrigued to be annoyed by it.

"So where are you going?" She asked, finally.

"Durham. It's in North Carolina."

"I never heard of it."

"It's in the east near Raleigh. That's where Duke University is."

She shrugged her shoulders. "Why are you going there?"

"Actually I'm going to Florida. I'm stopping in Durham on the way down to visit an old friend."

"Man friend or woman friend?"

"Actually both. My friend and his wife and they have two kids."

"Which one did you know first?"

I smiled at her. "Now why would you ask that?"

"Never mind. It's none of my business. It just changes what your visit is all about. In my mind I mean. It's not like I need to know or anything but if you don't tell me then I have to imagine what it means myself, and I could be completely wrong about it."

I laughed. "Are you trying to get into my head, already? I've only known you for five minutes. That's got to be a world's record."

"No. It just helps me understand who you are. You can't really tell what somebody's like by what they do. You need to know why. I meet a lot of people in the city and sometimes I need to make a judgment about them. My instincts about people are pretty good, but they're not perfect."

"Well, to answer your question, her name is Jennifer and we dated for a while back in high school. Walt is a friend of mine from college. So I guess I've known Jennifer longer but Walt is my friend. Is that complicated enough for you?"

"That's perfect. So are you just stopping by to catch up?"

"Something like that."

"How long since you saw him last?"

"Actually, it's been a long time. Three years maybe. He was up here on business. I kind of lost track of him for a while. You know how it is."

"Yeah. I've lost track of lots of people. Some of them just went away and a few of them died. Some of them just let go of their soul and it drifted away like smoke. Those are the worst. Their body is still there but there's nothing left inside."

I didn't know how to respond to that either. I'm sure it showed on my face because she looked away for a moment as if she were hiding. I started to say something but she didn't let me finish.

"So why are you going to Florida?"

"No real reason. I just felt like being someplace warm for a while."

"Are you going on vacation?"

"Sort of. I sold my business. I guess I'm just looking for a change of scenery."

She paused for a moment, and continued her exploration of my face.

"You should go somewhere else, Florida is no good."

"Why?"

"Because there's no magic there."

"There's the Magic Kingdom." I said, smiling.

"Do you actually like that place? I can't stand it. It's all so fake."

"You have to ignore that part and just pretend. It's about being a kid again."

"I guess, but anyway Florida is just a bummer."

"And you would know that how?"

"I've been there. It sucks. Too humid. Too many bugs. Too many old people. Too flat."

"But there's the ocean."

"Yeah, there's the ocean. But that's not enough. Not for me anyway."

I tried to change the subject.

"And where are you going?"

She took a long sip of her soda, and I could see she was considering her answer.

"Richmond."

"Why Richmond?"

"There's somebody there I need to see."

"Family?"

"No. I never met her before. It's complicated."

"So where were you living in the city?"

"I stayed with friends most of the time. I didn't have a place of my own."

It was obvious she didn't want to talk about it and I didn't press her further. Now it was her turn to be quiet for a while. I watched her eyes, taking in the constant parade of people, coming and going. Studying the faces. Watching the body language. Not uneasy perhaps, but watchful. I didn't interrupt her.

"So where do you live anyway?" She asked, still looking out across the room as she slowly turned her attention back to me.

"We lived in Rutland."

"That's in Vermont right? Skiing and stuff."

"Yeah that's where Killington is."

"Are you a skier?"

"Yeah. I like to ski."

"Are you good at it?"

"I'm okay. Not an expert, I don't do it enough to be really good."

"I never tried it, but it looks really cool. We used to go sledding in Central Park; only we didn't have a real sled so we used sheets of cardboard. It was fun."

"Did you grow up in New York?"

"Part of the time. Me and my mom lived in Macon for a little while. That's in Georgia. We moved back to New York when I was fourteen. She's dead now."

"I'm sorry to hear that."

"Yeah. I'm sorry too. I wasn't even there when she died. I went out to Ohio to stay with some friends for a while. We weren't getting along very well. She didn't like them and she was always trying to keep me from going out. I know she was just trying to look out for me, but at the time I felt like I was in jail or something. I guess I was a real brat. Anyway, I was gone for like six months. When I came back to New York she was already buried. I just wish I had been able to say goodbye, you know? I go and sit by her grave sometimes and talk to her. I don't know if she can hear me, but it makes me feel better. I used to sit on her lap and talk to her when I was little. Now it's like she's still there, only she's turned to stone."

Once again, I was at a loss for words. I was really a little stunned. She just sat there and stared at me. There was sadness in her eyes and for the first time since the conversation started, just a hint of vulnerability. It took me a few seconds to refocus.

"Didn't somebody try to get in touch with you to let you know?"

"I don't think so. We didn't have any family and I don't think anybody knew where I was. My mom told me she had a cousin living out in California somewhere, but I never met her. I didn't know how to get in touch with her."

"That must have been hard."

She shrugged her shoulders and looked out the window for a moment. When she looked back at me, the strain of it was all over her face. Like a child, pretending not to be afraid of the dark. I looked into her eyes and saw them go clear, like some kind of veil had been lifted. I felt like I was seeing her for the first time and I don't think she wasn't ready to show herself to me just yet. She immediately glanced away and changed the subject.

"Yeah, I cried a lot. But that's the way life is. So what kind of business did you have?"

"We manufactured metal assemblies."

"You mean like bridges and stuff?"

"No. Small assemblies."

"For what?"

"We built them to the customer's specifications."

"So you must be really smart right? Like and engineer or something."

"I'm a mechanical engineer."

"I suck at math. It just doesn't fit in my head right. I mean I can do the basic stuff but I tried to learn geometry once and it just wasn't happening. You know what I mean?"

"You would have gotten it eventually. You just need to stick with it."

The waitress returned with our orders. Megan turned her attention to the other diners as she ate.

"You see that guy over there at the counter?" She asked, nodding her head in the general direction. "He's some kind of cop."

"How do you know?"

"You can just see it. Watch him for a little while."

"I'll take your word for it."

"And that woman there with the two kids. The one with the red knitted hat. She just split up with her old man and she's taking the kids somewhere to get away from him."

I looked over at the woman and back at Megan again. I just shrugged my shoulders. She looked back at me waiting for some response but I didn't want to challenge her. It seemed to me she was probing for my edges. Revealing herself to me at a measured pace as she tried to define the space we were suddenly occupying together. Seeing how far I was willing to walk with her before I wanted to come back to someplace safe. The waitress came over again.

"You want another soda, sweetie?"

"My name is Megan. No thanks, anyway."

She looked over at me again. Watching as I finished off my coffee.

"You have nice hands. They're strong but they're not rough looking. Do you plan an instrument?"

"No. I used to play around on the guitar but I was never much good at it. How about you?"

"No. I can sing a little, but I'm not that good at it either."

"So you know a lot about people?" I asked, changing the subject.

"I like to look at people and figure out what's going on with them. Sometimes I sit in the park for hours just watching. It's much better than television. It's like everyone is in their own little world. They're absent, you know? Some of them are just drifting and some are going around their own private star. Everybody's looking for something. Most of them don't even know what it is. You're a little different though. You're present. That's what I saw."

"You mean when you asked who I was?"

"Who you are. It doesn't matter who you were."

"Do you have it figured out now?"

"Enough."

"Enough for what?"

She shrugged her shoulders.

"Do you want anything else?"

"No, I'm fine, thanks a lot."

I slid a few bills under the edge of my plate and then stood and put my jacket on. Her eyes were locked on me, unblinking. I assumed she was in need of a ride and I didn't think she wanted to come out and ask me directly. I decided to make it easy on her.

"So what now? Do you need a lift?"

"Yes. But only if you want to. I can always get a ride."

"Sure. I'll be going through Richmond anyway. I'd enjoy the company."

The woman in the red hat was in front of us as we walked toward the lobby. The little girl looked up at her and said, 'when is daddy coming'? Megan leaned over and whispered.

"See. I told you so."

We walked out to my car and I unlocked the door for her. She put her backpack on the floor and climbed up onto the passenger seat. The sky was darker now, and it looked like there was going to be some weather. She shivered and as we pulled out onto the highway I turned the heater up for her. I felt a little awkward then, suddenly alone with her in the car. Like we somehow needed to start the conversation all over again. She was just staring out the side window, gone into her own world. Close enough to touch, but a million miles away. Finally, she turned to me and stared until I looked over at her. She had a solemn expression on her face.

"So, do you want to know what happened?"

"What do you mean?"

"I mean why I'm going to Richmond."

"Sure if you want to tell me."

2

She took a water bottle out of the side pocket of her backpack and took a long, deliberate drink. As she put it away she gave me a sideways glance and then resumed her study of the scenery. She started talking without looking at me again.

"So, are you sure you want to hear about it? About how I got here I mean. It's a little odd. At least I think it is."

"I'm okay with odd."

She was silent for another moment but then she leapt into it without taking a breath. The words bursting forth like waves washing up on a beach.

"Okay, well it all started because of the necklace. I was hanging out with this guy George who was in a band, except they weren't that good and he had to pawn his amp to pay the rent. It's not like they couldn't play or anything. It's just that they played the same crap everybody else plays. You need your own style if you want to make it in music. In art too. Anyway, this was a few years ago. So they got this gig and I went with him to the pawn shop to get his amp back. While I was waiting I was looking around the store, you know, and I saw this necklace in the display case. It was a little girl on a bicycle. She had this little round hat with ribbons hanging down the back and she was wearing a little dress, like a smock. Later on I found out the little girl was supposed to be Madeline from those kid's books. I saw them over at the library one day when I was looking for pictures of animals. The books I mean. I draw, you know, like caricatures and stuff. That's how I make money, except I don't make a lot. I was taking art classes for a while, but I couldn't afford it anymore. I love art, especially paintings. I love the Dutch painters most of all. Like Rembrandt. His faces are more real than photographs. It's like their souls are shining out through their skin. I could look at them for hours. Sometimes I go over to the museum and spend the whole day there trying to draw the way they did."

She paused, and looked out the side window at some people standing by a car with a flat tire.

"That sucks. Anyway, the necklace was silver and I really loved it but the tag said thirty five bucks and I only had twenty. The guy wouldn't sell it to me so I left, but for some reason it was eating away at me. I'm not usually like that with 'things' but I just had to have that necklace. So the next day I went back with my sketch pad and I told the guy I would draw his picture if he would sell me the necklace for fifteen dollars. He said. 'What happened to the twenty dollars you were offering me yesterday'? So I told him I had to eat some of it, and he said okay. So I drew a caricature of this guy, and I made his nose look a little like a dick because I thought he was a dickhead for not selling me the necklace for twenty bucks in the first place."

I looked over at her and laughed. She grinned back at me briefly, and then launched herself back into her story.

"I figured he would throw me out of the store, but he liked it. I guess he secretly liked being a dickhead. That's a funny thing I do with caricatures. I try to capture a little of what I think the person is like inside. It's really

26

amazing. Like if I think somebody is a little mean, that's how I draw them and they love it. I draw people looking nice too, if I think they are. I'd like to draw you. So anyway I got the necklace and I put it on and I never took it off again for almost three years. Which is why I almost freaked when she told me it used to be hers."

"Who told you?"

"The old woman in the park. But I didn't get to that part yet."

She took off her slippers and put her feet up on the dash. She was wearing a pair of multi-colored toe socks. A couple of the toes were missing and her own toes were sticking out. I looked over at her socks and smiled.

"Is this okay? She asked."

"Sure, I don't mind."

"I haven't been in a car for like a year or something. I mean before today. Some guy I know gave me a ride to the rest stop."

She pulled down the visor and looked at herself in the mirror. She was trying to rearrange her hair but after a while she gave up and resumed staring out the window. She was beginning to relax and I didn't want to break the spell. I wasn't really sure how to react to her anyway. After a while she glanced over at me and continued her story.

"So, I'm not crazy or anything like that, but I have something called Tourette's syndrome. At least I'm pretty sure I do. There isn't any test for it. People with Tourettes have twitches and things and sometimes they make strange sounds and blurt things out. They can't help it. Sometimes they make these really nasty comments and it freaks people out. I don't do anything like that but sometimes I just say stuff to people. It's like the stuff that comes into your head when you see somebody, only you don't say it because you don't want to hurt their feelings. Well I say it. It just comes out and I can't stop it. That's why I have trouble keeping a job. I worked in this really cool bookstore for a while and I really loved it, but I kept insulting the customers and they fired me. Like one day this really fat woman came in. I mean she could hardly fit through the door. She waddled up to the counter and instead of saying 'May I help you,' like I was supposed to, I said. 'Wow, you must have the biggest butt in New York.' So anyway, if I say something to you that seems mean, it's not because I want to. Anyway it usually doesn't happen with people I like, and I like you. At least so far."

"Well thank you."

She nodded and gave me a quick glance before leaping back into it.

"So anyway I was over in the park one day by the Guggenheim. I know some of the guards there. I drew caricatures of them and they let me in for free sometimes if their boss isn't around. There was this exposition of Russian art but I didn't like it much. Those people are like permanently bummed out. I walked over to the park and I was sitting on a bench and watching the people skating and walking their dogs and stuff when this old woman walked by. She looked well off, the way she was dressed and all, but later I found out she wasn't. Anyway, she looked at me and then she stopped and did like a double-take. She walked over and leaned down and took a real long look at my necklace. I was kind of freaked, you know, but for once I didn't say anything and then she sat down next to me and said, 'could I ask you where you got that necklace?' So I told her and she asked me if it had an inscription on the back and I told her it did. Before I could tell her what it said she told me! 'It says Annie 2/25/39'. I guess my jaw must have dropped. She said that the necklace had once been hers. She told me this whole story about how her father had been a rare book collector and he used to travel to Europe all the time. They were Jewish and when he traveled to Germany a few months after he gave her the necklace, he was picked up by the Nazis and they never saw him again. She told me the necklace was the last thing he had ever given her and she had lost it when their house burned down a few years later. It was just so sad. She asked me if she could touch it and she started to cry. For some reason I just felt so close to her at that moment and so I took off the necklace and I gave it to her and told her she could have it back. It was really strange. I loved that necklace so much and while I was giving it to her a little voice in my mind was complaining at me but I had to do it, you know? I wouldn't have been able to wear it after that. Can I roll the window down a little? I like the air."

"Sure, go ahead."

She was quiet for a while and her eyes were closed as she leaned over close to the window to let the wind wash over her face. She had returned again to her far-away place. After a few minutes, she sat back and opened her eyes again. She took a couple of deep breaths and then stretched her arms out in front of her. Her head almost disappeared into her jacket.

"Wow, I forgot how good that feels."

After a few moments, she gathered herself and continued.

"So anyway this woman, Annabel, tells me she doesn't have much money to pay for the necklace, but she invites me to her apartment for lunch, and I thought, what the hell, you know? I really didn't want to take any money for it anyway. It just didn't feel right. So we walked over to her place. It was in this really beautiful old building on the Upper East Side. Her place was on the second floor. I guess it was rent-controlled because if was in this up-scale neighborhood and it didn't sound like she had the money for it. Her apartment was amazing. It was like a museum inside. It was like somebody decorated it a hundred years ago and never changed a thing. There were tons of old books and a bunch of other neat stuff in there, like old oil lamps and stuff, and I just walked around and looked at it all while she made some soup and sandwiches for us. We ate and she told me what it was like growing up in New York. She said they were hard times but her family had a little bit of money, more than a lot of people and it sounded like she really had fun. I wish I could go back to those times. Not forever, just for a day or something and just walk around and do some of

31

the stuff she told me about. I was really enjoying myself and then after we were done eating I helped her clear the table and then she asked me to sit on the couch because she wanted to get something. She went into her bedroom and she came back with a little ring box. She sat down next to me on the couch and she opened it. There was this beautiful ring inside. This one here."

She held her hand out for me. It was a fine gold band shaped like a vine, embedded with small leaf-shaped green stones.

"It's really nice; I noticed it in the restaurant."

"Yeah, I love it and you know what? It's worth like a hundred times more than the necklace ever was. She told me it had been given to her by a suitor. That's what she called him, a suitor. She said she really didn't like the guy all that much and they split up a few months later but he let her keep the ring. She said she wanted me to have it. I didn't even pretend not to want it. But then things got a little weird. She asked me if she could hold my hand, and I was like, well that's a little strange but okay. So then she tells me she can see things. Not with everybody but with some people, like if she touches them she can see things from their past and sometimes from their future. So I thought, cool. Anyway she holds my hand for a long time and she closes her eyes and after a few minutes I thought she had fallen asleep because her eyes were twitching and stuff, but I just sat there real still, just looking at her. Finally she opened her eyes and she smiled at me with this really loving smile, like a mother smiling at her daughter. And I smiled back and asked her what she saw. She didn't answer right away. She got up and put the tea kettle on and got some cups out of the cupboard, and I was like staring at her, you know, dying to know what she saw. Finally I asked her again, and she says 'I saw quite a lot, but let me pour the tea and then I'll tell you'."

"So she comes back with the tea on this little silver tray with some cookies and she puts it on the table, and then she looks at me and says, 'there is a strong connection between us. Can you tell me your mother's name'? So I tell her my mother was Elizabeth Doyle but she died a few years back and she looks at me and nods. And then she tells me she knew my mother. She says my mother was just a little girl at the time and she was a teenager, but they would play together sometimes. So, I think she's shining me on, until she tells me my mother had a mole shaped like a heart on her upper left thigh, and I like almost fell on the floor. Then she says it was no accident that we met as we did. She said that most of the time people meet for no real reason. It's just random. But sometimes people meet because they need to help each other in some way. She tells me she had been having these vivid dreams about her father for like weeks and she felt this strong need to connect with his spirit in some way, and forces that no one understood brought us together in the park. I was like whoa, this is really freaky, like I don't even know if I can even handle this, but I just kept quiet. Then she says there were some things she needed to talk to me about. She tells me it's time for me to leave New York. She says there is no more for me to learn in the city and the longer I stay, the more dangerous it will become for me. She says there are already people near to me who would do me harm if I stay, which really freaks me out even more. So I say, how can I leave New York? I don't have any money and where would I go anyway. She told me I would find a way and she started to cry and I wasn't sure what to do so I just gave her a hug and she held on to me for a long time. Finally she pulled away and she looked at me and I thought she would be sad but she was like smiling through her tears. She asked me how she could get in touch with me. I gave her a friend's phone number and then I left."

She pulled her feet off of the dash and curled them under her. The rain was coming down harder and she rolled the window back up and took another drink from the water bottle. A semi flew past and it rocked the car. She shook her head.

"What an asshole. He's going to kill somebody driving like that. Do you want to hear the rest, I'm almost done?"

"Of course!"

"So all of this happened a couple of weeks ago and I was pretty freaked out for a couple of days, like really paranoid but then I just kind of forgot about it. I've been staying with a friend named Rick for the last couple of months. He's an artist and he got a job at a little church over on 42nd St. He gets to live there for free and he sleeps in this little loft in the back. All he has to do is kind of clean up after the services and keep an eye on the place so nobody breaks in. The minister calls him his sexton which is pretty funny because that's mostly what he does. He has a ton of sex with all these girls in that loft and in the pews and all over the church. All except for me. We have an understanding. I just help him with the place and I sleep there, that's it. Anyway, about a week after I met Annabel, Rick tells me his friend Chuck is going to be staying with him for a few days but it's all cool and Chuck is a good guy. But when I meet him I get this really bad vibe from him and it made me a little nervous but I didn't have any other place to stay."

"That night, Rick and Chuck got into drinking and smoking some weed and they wanted me to get into it with them. I had a little wine but that was it. They were really going at it and after a while I just crashed on one of the cots. I woke up later and this guy Chuck was all over me. I told him no, but he got really rough and he started hitting me and trying to take my clothes off. I was screaming but Rick was like passed out and I didn't know what to do, so I pretended to go along with it. So this guy Chuck starts getting all tender and crap, kissing me on my neck and like I wanted to vomit. I just went along with it for a while but I was looking for something to hit him with. I finally managed to get out from under him and there was this big brass crucifix thing on the shelf and I grabbed it and I smashed him across the face with it. He went down like he was dead and I was afraid I killed him, but I found out later he just had a concussion and he was going to be all right. I was really glad, even though he was a complete asshole. I never want to really hurt anyone, you know? So I ran out of the church but it was the middle of the night and I didn't know where to go. It was pouring rain. I ended up in this alley over by Third Avenue wrapped in an old smelly blanket I found. It was disgusting but I was cold. I couldn't sleep because I was shivering so bad and there were rats. I cried all night because I thought I might have killed somebody. All night I was thinking about what Annabel said and I decided I had to leave whether I had any money or not."

"The next morning, as soon as the sun came up I got up and left the alley, and this is the really weird part. I was walking over all this trash and I was being really careful because of the used needles and broken glass and stuff that I didn't even see the night before. Then I noticed this envelope in a plastic bag and it looked like it had something in it. I opened it and there was like more than three hundred dollars in there. There was no name or anything so I figured that was the money Annabel told me I would find. Isn't that weird? I mean I never really believed in that kind of stuff before. There has to be a thousand old women in New York that call themselves psychics but it's mostly just crap. But Annabel, I don't know what to think about her."

I looked over at her. I was a little skeptical but I didn't want to hurt her feelings, so I just nodded my head.

"I know it sounds strange but it's true, I swear. Look, I'll show you." She reached into her backpack and pulled out a grimy envelope stuffed with bills.

"You wouldn't take this from me would you?"

"No of course not."

"I mean, I can pay you for the lunch you bought for me and the tolls or something. I don't mind."

"I don't need your money, but why did you ask me to buy you lunch if you had money of your own?"

"Because I needed to see what kind of guy you were. I mean, I was pretty sure you were a good person, but I had to know for sure before I let you give me a ride."

"And how did you know I would give you a ride?"

"I don't know. I just did."

She stopped talking then and started arranging things in her backpack. I waited for her to start up again but she seemed to be lost in her thoughts. Finally, I broke the silence.

"So what happened, did you leave right away after you found the money?"

"Well I was going to, but I went over to my friend's apartment to take a shower and there was a message there from Annabel. I went over to see her that afternoon and she seemed really different. She was nervous and upset and I asked her what was wrong but she wouldn't tell me. She made some tea for me and after a while she seemed to calm down a little. She started telling me about her family and how they were all gone and she didn't have anyone left in the world and how lonely that made her feel. I felt really sad and I told her I could come over to see her any time she wanted. She hugged me again, and then she said something really strange. She said she didn't have much time left and there was something she wanted me to have. I asked her what it was but all she would tell me was it was something that would help me to start a new life. She gave me the name and address of a woman in Richmond and told me to go meet her and she would explain everything. Then she opened up her purse and tried to give me some money to buy a train ticket, but I didn't want to take it. I spent the rest of the day with her, and when I left she just said 'I'm so glad I finally found you'. Isn't that strange? I mean, I can't figure the whole thing out, but that's why I'm going to Richmond."

"And you don't have any idea what she's giving you?"

"No, she wouldn't tell me for some reason. The whole thing is just really odd. It seemed like she really wanted me to get out of the city and after what happened with that guy Chuck, I figured she was right. It was really starting to creep me out."

"How come you didn't take the train?"

"I don't know. I think maybe it's because when I'm on a train I feel like I'm stuck some place with a bunch of people I don't know, and it's moving and I can't get away. At least in the city I knew where I was and if somebody was bothering me I knew where to go."

"Do people bother you a lot?"

"Pretty much. I think it's because I don't have my own place and people think they can get over on me. Especially guys. I don't trust guys too much.   Especially young guys. I trust you though."

"Why?"

"Because I can pretty much tell what somebody is like if I spend a little time with them."

"Well some people are pretty good at hiding who they really are."

"Yeah, but I can tell. I don't know how, but I usually know. I don't get fooled too often. In the beginning I used to, but not so much any more."

3

We crossed the Delaware River near Wilmington late in the afternoon. By then we had arrived at a workable silence, not entirely comfortable but easier than digging too far into things. Anything more would require the breaching of barriers and the opening of doors to private places. I didn't see any point in laying myself open any more than I already had. I was more than a little surprised at how much I had told her as it was. It's curious, how some people can open you like a book and get you to reveal things about yourself that you wouldn't discuss with your closest friends. Maybe it's because they're not part of your life, and you don't have to live with the unspoken judgments and silent recriminations. Still, there are things better considered in the light.

She had drifted back into her own thoughts and didn't seem eager to talk either. I had never met anyone like Megan and I found myself wanting to understand her. It seemed to me she didn't deserve the hand life had dealt her and I wanted to know why. I also knew, by then, that the only way I would find out any more would be for her to reveal it to me voluntarily. We were driving through the leading edge of a nor'easter moving up the eastern seaboard. The wipers were virtually useless and it felt like the wind was about to blow us off into the bay. I looked over at her and I could see the concern on her face. The bad weather and the growing darkness made the car feel a little claustrophobic. It had also occurred to me that there was no way we were going to reach Richmond unless we drove through the night. We would need to find a place to sleep, and that was an entirely new conversation that I wasn't ready for. I was hungry and I needed to stretch my legs. I was about to suggest we take a break, but before I could say anything, she asked if we could stop at the next rest area so she could use the bathroom.

It took us another hour to reach it. We grabbed some pizza at the Sbarro and then ran back out to the car. It was completely dark now and the rain had not subsided. It was going to be another five hours to Richmond, even if the traffic was moving, which it wasn't. When I pulled back out onto the highway it was almost at a standstill. I kept at if for another hour but right after we crossed over into Maryland the traffic had ceased to move at all. I flipped on the radio and searched for a local station. I found a news channel and they were warning motorists to avoid Rte. 95 southbound near Baltimore due to a massive wreck that was blocking all three lanes. The police were making traffic exit at Havre de Grace. It didn't look promising. I looked over at Megan who had managed to doze off. She looked like a child, wrapped up in her oversized jacket with her head against the glass. She seemed so helpless. I wondered again how in the world she had survived so long in a place like New York. In a while, I spotted an exit and just managed to get into the right lane in time. There was a motel at the end of the off ramp and I pulled in and parked in front of the office. Megan stirred and sat up.

"Where are we?"

"I had to pull off the highway. There's a big accident up ahead. Listen, we're not going to make it to Richmond tonight the way things are going. Even if we get there it'll be too late to visit anyone. I thought we might as well spend the night somewhere and get a fresh start in the morning. This place looks as good as any."

She looked out the window at the motel but said nothing.

"Look, you don't have to worry. I'll get you your own room."

She looked over at me and smiled.

"Why, are you afraid I'll attack you or something?"

"No, I just thought you would be uncomfortable sharing a room with a stranger."

"You're not a stranger. I know you a little now. Besides, I would rather be with somebody tonight. It's the first I've been out of the city for a really long time and I feel a little strange. Just get a room with two beds, Okay? I know you wouldn't hurt me."

It was a standard-issue roadside motel room. Two, swayback double beds, a television, and matching burgundy drapes and bedspreads with a nondescript geometric pattern. A washed-out landscape print was screwed onto the wall above the dresser. The carpet was grimy and a bit frayed but the room looked clean. There were a few water stains on the spackled ceiling. Megan went immediately to the bathroom and checked it out.

"Would you mind if I took a shower?"

"Go right ahead."

I kicked off my shoes and stretched out on the bed nearest the door. The news was on and I watched absently, not really paying attention. In a moment she peaked her head back into the room.

"I'm not a prostitute."

I just looked at her, not sure how to respond.

"I didn't think you were." I said finally, "You don't need to worry about me."

"I'm not worried. I just wanted you to know that about me."

She stood there studying me for a moment and then she disappeared again. In a while I heard the shower start and after a minute or so I could hear her singing. She had a good voice. A voice that fit her body and she could carry a tune quite well. I turned down the television for a moment and listened to her. It made me smile. It was amazing to me that someone with so little, without even a roof over her head and living such a tenuous existence, could be so apparently happy. I couldn't shake the image of her sitting alone in the dark in some filthy, rat infested alley. Whatever her secrets, she didn't deserve that. In any case, I was glad to have a traveling companion, even for a short while. When I had first considered going to Florida, the long drive alone was not something I looked forward to. But I wasn't going back. The house was sold. The furniture was in storage and I was looking for a new start. Looking forward to putting it all behind me. I wasn't sure Florida was where I wanted to live, but I had access to a condo in Boca Raton for as long as I wanted to use it. It belonged to my former business partner who was traveling in Europe. It seemed like a good place to sort things out.

She was gone for nearly an hour but I had long ago learned never to question how much time a woman needed in the bathroom. Finally, the door opened and she emerged in a cloud of steam. She was dressed in a pair of men's pajamas that were also too large for her. They were rolled at the wrists and ankles and cinched at the waist with what looked like a piece of clothesline. Her head was swaddled in a towel like a sultan's turban giving her the look of a genie from the Arabian Nights. She gave me a sideways glance and then sat at the end of the bed, aimlessly arranging things in her backpack. More vulnerable now that something domestic had passed between us.

"Don't you own any clothes that fit?" I asked, laughing.

"These fit just fine. They leave lots of room for my dreams."

I smiled back at her and tossed her the remote.

"My turn." I grabbed some things from my suitcase and went into the bathroom. The mirror was still steamed over and I noticed she had washed her underwear and it was hanging on the shower rod. For a moment it was like I had traveled back in time, to when Ann and I were away on one of our skiing vacations. A feeling of emptiness started to wash over me but I pushed back at it, determined not to let it take hold. It had smothered me for too long and I knew it was time to bury it for good. She wasn't coming back. Nothing could be undone. Nothing could be unsaid. I couldn't trade places with her, even though sometimes I wished I could. I was still alive and determined to do something more with my life. I just didn't know what it was. When I came out of the bathroom, I was happy to see her, sitting cross-legged on the bed, flipping through the channels. I sat on the other bed and watched her. She looked over at me and smiled. She was flipping through the channels so fast that there was no time for a full image to settle on the screen.

"What are you doing?"

"I'm watching TV."

"Don't you think it would be better if you settled on one of the channels and actually watched something?"

"No, I hate television. I never watch it. There's so much crap on there it's unbelievable. But I like the patterns. If you flip the channels real fast you get some really neat effects. It's kind of like modern art. If you do it for a while the patterns start to make sense a little. Like they're telling a story that nobody ever wrote. It's sort of out of you and in you at the same time. This one switches a little slow though."

She kept at it for a few more moments and then she switched it off. There were a few seconds of awkward silence, as we both stared at the gray screen, not knowing what was supposed to come next.

"Could I ask you something?" I said, after a few moments.

"Sure."

"You said you knew I wouldn't hurt you. How could you know that?"

"Why? Was I wrong?"

"No. I just can't help thinking that if the roles were reversed I wouldn't be so confident."

"Well, how do you know you're safe with me? Just because you're bigger and stronger?"

"It never crossed my mind."

"You don't know me either. I could be a homicidal maniac for all you know. I could be a serial killer."

"I don't see that in you."

"Most people wouldn't see it until it was too late. You might though. You're a little different. Most people like you are too wrapped up in their lives to be that aware. My friend Chris calls it the wall of expectations."

"How do you mean?"

"It's like there's an invisible wall between your world and mine. Most of the time it keeps people like you safe. You live your life expecting that everything is going to be like it always was except a little better. Even when you come into the city you're still safe behind your wall. It's a different city for people like you. It's taxis and doormen and head waiters. The cops take people like you seriously. They just want us to go away. Sometimes you get mugged or hassled a little, but for the most part you're safe. Sometimes, college kids come into the city looking for dope. They step across the wall. Sometimes they don't go home. On my side of the wall, nobody's safe, ever. Everybody's surviving, minute to minute. Day to day. It sharpens your senses. I've heard that some mystics call it the third eye. It lets you see inside of things. Inside of people. Some can see the light around people and they can read them by it. Some just have a feeling they get when they're close to danger. I could see you almost right away."

"What did you see?"

"I saw kindness and sadness. I saw someone who was pretty much in the moment, which is a rare thing with you grillers."

"Grillers?"

"People from the other side of the wall. That's what we call you, among other things."

"Why grillers?"

"You know. Barbecues. That kind of crap. The stuff you do with other people who have money. After you mow the lawn. Grillers are all wrapped up in whatever drama they're going through. I've really never lived on your side of the wall but it looks exhausting. Worrying about all of your stuff and about your careers and your retirement and college for the kids and trying to impress each other. It closes you off. We don't have stuff. At least not much of it. Like Dylan said in the 60's. 'If you ain't got nothin, you got nothin to lose'."

"So you look down on us?"

"Not really. I'm sure it's nice to be safe. I just don't know if it's worth living behind a wall. Everything I own fits in my backpack. It's easy to carry and not much to lose."

"So you don't want any more out of life than you have in that backpack?"

"Well sure. I mean there are things I'd like to have. Like a place of my own to live in, for one thing. But I don't have expectations. I take my life as it is every day. If something good happens, I'm happy about it. I just don't sit around feeling bad that I don't have more. I don't feel sorry for myself. I believe there's a reason I'm here and my life is what it is. I just haven't found out what it is yet. For a while I thought it was because of the way I lived my past lives. Like a punishment or something. But I don't think that way any more. I think whatever life you have is designed to help you learn something. To change your real self in some way. The part of you that carries on from life to life. What everybody calls your soul."

"So you believe in reincarnation."

"It's the only thing that really makes any sense to me. My mother was a Catholic and she believed there was a place called heaven where you go if you're good. It's supposed to be this place where you're happy all the time just hanging out with God. That doesn't make a lot of sense to me. I don't think we were created to just sit around. We need to be doing things. So, anyway, I just live my life. I trust my instincts about people and then I just let life happen. I'm not worried about being alone with you. If I was, I wouldn't be here in the first place."

"Well that's a pretty good attitude for anyone."

"I guess. Anyway, what do you want to do now?"

"Well, I was going to watch TV but I guess that's out."

"No, you can watch it if you want. I don't mind if it's on."

She threw the remote over to me.

"What are you going to do?"

"I'm going to draw."

"What are you going to draw?"

"You."

"What. Do I have to pose or something?"

"No, just pretend I'm not here."

She leaned off the end of the bed and grabbed her backpack. She had a sketch book inside and a little, plastic case with pencils and charcoal. I turned the TV back on and flipped through the channels until I found a nature show. I glanced over at her briefly but she was deep in concentration. I had thought it would feel a little odd, sharing a room with someone I didn't really know, but it didn't feel that way at all. After a while, I almost forgot she was there. I was lost in the program when she threw a pencil over at me to get my attention.

"I'm finished. Do you want to see it?"

"Sure."

I was expecting some kind of cartoon but when she passed the sketchbook over to me, I was stunned. It was a drawing of me behind the wheel of my Explorer and it was so well done it looked like it belonged on a wall in a museum.

"Wow." I said, looking over at her. "This is really terrific. I had no idea you were this good."

"I can do better. I didn't know you very well when I took that picture."

"What do you mean, when you took the picture?"

"I don't know. It's the way I see things. I can't really explain it. It's like I take snapshots in my head, without a camera. Not all the time, that would be really confusing. It's like when I'm with someone there is one moment when I really see the person. You know? Not just with my eyes, but with my heart. I never know when it is going to happen, but when it does my mind takes a picture and I can draw it later on."

"That's amazing. I never heard of anything like that before."

"Yeah, I guess it's a thing. I only ever met one other person who could do it but he was into porno."

"You really aught to do something with your talent. I think you could make a lot of money with this."

"It isn't that easy, really. I know a lot of talented artists. To really make money you need to be discovered by one of those stiff-assed gallery owners. It's really political. The museums won't hang you until after you're dead for a while. I make more money with my cartoons than I do with this stuff. I'd be better off framing a lump of dog shit with a gum wrapper stuck in it. That would probably sell for thousands."

I laughed. "Well don't give up on it. You are really very good. Sooner or later someone is going to give you a break."

"We'll see. So anyway, what do you want to do know? Are you done watching TV?"

"There's not much on."

"Do you want to go to sleep then. I don't mind."

"No it's still pretty early. I'd like to find out more about you, though, about what your life is like."

"Why?"

"Because I've never met anyone like you before. I guess I don't understand how you get by."

"It's not as hard as you think. I know a lot of people in the city. It's like we're all a family and we help each other. Most of us don't have any money but we do things for each other. Like I know this gay couple. They actually do have some money and they travel a lot. When they're going out of town, I stay at their apartment and I do their laundry and clean up the place. They always leave plenty of food in the fridge and I stay there while they're gone."

"How do they know how to find you without a phone?"

"There's always somebody who knows where you are. It's like we're all connected. The word gets around. There are a lot of places I can crash for a night or two. It's like that. I make some money with my cartoons and that's how I pay for food and for the things I need."

"Don't you worry about being so exposed all the time?"

"That's what everyone thinks when they find out you're homeless. The thing is, everybody knows we don't have anything worth stealing. I can go places where you couldn't."

"What about being attacked?"

"You mean raped?"

"That too."

"Well most of the robberies are done by junkies looking for a fix. Most of them couldn't get it up if they tried, and you could knock them over with a dirty look. Besides, they'd rather shoot up than screw anyway."

"Okay, but there must be psycho's out on the street."

"Yeah. There's that, but that's true for people like you too. Anyway, a lot of that has to do with fate. It has to do with whether it's your time. If it isn't, somebody will get in the way."

"What do you mean by that?"

"Just what I said."

"You believe that's true?"

"I know it is."

"How?"

"Because it's happened to me."

"Really? What happened?"

She paused for a moment and just stared at me. After a few seconds she shook her head.

"Look, I don't want to be rude, but I'm not ready for that conversation yet and I don't have the energy for it right now. I think I'd like to get some sleep now. Is that okay?"

"Sure."

"Good night then, and thanks a lot for helping me. I really do appreciate it."

With that she climbed under her covers and turned away from me. I just sat there staring at her for a moment, completely amazed at this person who had just stepped into my life. And then I said good night and turned off the lights.

4

Megan was still asleep when I awoke the next morning. It looked like she hadn't moved the entire night and she was so still I had to watch her for a moment to make sure she was still breathing. I shaved and had a quick shower. When I emerged she was already dressed. She mumbled good morning and then went into the bathroom while I got myself ready. The motel had a continental breakfast set up in the lobby and we both ate a little. Megan wasn't speaking and she wasn't making much eye-contact either. When we were done, I grabbed another coffee for the road and we headed out to the car. It was a chilly morning and she stood with her chin buried in her jacket and her arms wrapped around herself, shifting from foot to foot until I opened her door.

"Brrrr, turn the heater up would you."

"It's only going to blow cold air until the engine heats up."

"That's okay. At least it'll sound warm."

We drove south in an awkward silence. Megan seemed to be struggling with something and it was obvious she didn't want to talk about it. I decided not to push. When we got to the Baltimore tunnel, she sat up straight and made a funny face at me.

"Does this thing go under water? Jesus, I hate these things."

She was chewing at her fingernails by the time we reached the other end. We were almost at the Washington Beltway before she started talking again.

"That wasn't the only reason. What I told you about that guy Chuck and spending that night in the alley."

"The only reason for what?"

"The only reason I wanted to get out of the city."

She had that look on her face again, like she was afraid I wasn't going to believe her.

"Why else then?"

"I think somebody was following me."

"Are you sure?"

"Pretty sure."

"What makes you think so?"

"Well, after I visited Annabel the first time, I started noticing this creepy looking guy. I mean there are plenty of creepy looking guys in the city. Most of them are harmless. But this guy was different creepy. He was nasty creepy."

"How do you know he was different?"

"Because he came up to me on the street one time and he looked right at me and he had this look on his face that was mean and cruel. He was foreign, like from Egypt or Iraq or something. He had dead eyes."

"Did he say anything to you?"

"No, he just kind of smirked at me and then he laughed this cold laugh. It really freaked me out."

"And you saw him again, after that?"

"Yeah. I started seeing him everywhere. One night I was at my friends place and I woke up in the middle of the night and I looked out onto the street and he was there, across the street staring up at me. My whole body went cold. Another time he followed me down into the subway and he tried to grab my backpack."

"Did he ever try to stop you or talk to you?"

"No, only that one time and he didn't say anything to me. That's what makes it even worse. It was like he was getting ready to do something but he wanted to scare me to death first."

"Maybe that's all he was trying to do. Scare you."

"I don't know. I don't think so. After that night when I saw him out the window, my friend's apartment was broken into and they trashed the place. They emptied out all the drawers and pulled everything out of the closets but my friend said they didn't take anything. It's the first time I was really a little afraid in the city. I started not going around by myself, especially at night. I never thought I'd say this, but I'm glad I'm out of there now."

"Was that what you were talking about last night? About psychos?"

"No. I mean he is one, for sure. But I meant when you're really in trouble. When you get yourself jammed up and you're not in control any more. When you really are in danger."

"And that's happened to you?"

"Yeah. More than once."

"And you said someone got in the way."

"Yeah?"

"Who was it?"

She stared at me for a moment and then started to say something. Her lips started to move but no sound was coming out. She looked away again. I didn't say anything. I just waited.

"Okay, I'm going to tell you this but you're probably going to think I'm making it all up, and I'm not. It really happened."

"What really happened?"

"Three times, that I can remember, I was in some kind of trouble and some guy showed up out of nowhere and helped me.

"Is it somebody you know?"

"No. It's not even the same guy. It was a different guy every time."

"How did they help you?"

"Well, that's the really strange part. They really didn't do anything. They just showed up and talked to me and then everything was okay. I don't really know how to explain it."

"When did it first happen?"

"It was right after my mom died. I was really freaked out for a while and I wasn't thinking very clearly about anything. She didn't have much money. The people at the bank said there was enough to bury her but after that there wasn't much left. There wasn't enough for me to get an apartment or anything. I had enough to eat and stuff. For a while anyway, and I was making some money with my drawings. The thing is, I didn't really have any close friends anymore either and I was really lonely and kind of scared. So I was over in Soho one night at one of the galleries and I met this guy. He was an artist and he seemed really cool and we talked for a long time. He had some paintings in the show and they were like really dark and all, but there was a lot of that style back then. They were really good.

At least I thought they were. He asked me to come back to his place with him, just to talk and hang out. So I was like, sure, why not. So he tells me to wait there because he has to go talk to someone for a minute."

"Anyway I'm standing there and all of a sudden this other guy walks up to me. He was an older guy like fifty or something and he looked at me and he smiled and then he put his hand on my shoulder and, like that would normally have pissed me off, except it didn't. This feeling came over me. Like this warm feeling, and then the guy says, 'Don't go with him'. And I was like, what? And he says, that man you were just talking to. You should stay away from him. And I didn't know what to say but just then I saw this guy, the artist I was talking to, walking toward me and it was really strange. I looked at his face and I could just see there was something wrong with him. I don't know why I didn't see it before. I mean I must have been talking to him for an hour or something. Then I turned around and the old guy was gone. I mean I didn't see him walking away or anything, and that freaked me out even more. So this guy says, okay lets go, but I just said I can't and I left. I don't know if he followed me or not because when I got outside I ran. That's really strange right? I mean I know it could have been a coincidence. Maybe he knew

66

the artist and he knew he was a bad guy. That's what I thought at first. Anyway, a few months after that I saw this artist guy's picture in the newspaper and he was being charged with raping like five women or something and he killed one of them. That old guy probably saved my life. I didn't know what to think. Maybe it was because of how I felt when he touched me. There was something about his eyes too. It's like there was a light in there but really far away. Like when you look into a lake and see the reflection of a star. I thought about it a lot for a while, but eventually I just forgot about him. I forgot about him until it happened again."

"What happened?"

"I got in trouble again. I was hanging out with this guy Jose'. I didn't know it at the time but he was like a small-time drug dealer. So we were going to a party up in Washington Heights and he tells me we have to meet somebody with a car and they're going to drive us to pick up some more people he knew. I found out later he was really there to pick up some weed and pills he was going to sell at the party. So he takes me back into the creepy alley and I'm kind of afraid to be back there because it wasn't a good neighborhood and we have to wait for this car to show up. After about twenty minutes this car comes driving up the alley with its lights off and then the driver flashes his lights and keeps on going. About five minutes later he comes by again and does the same thing and Jose' waves to him. So I say 'Jose', what the hell is going on?' and he says it's okay, he'll stop the next time. And I was just about to ask him again when I see this other guy come walking up the alley. When he got closer, I couldn't believe what I was seeing. He looked so out of place I felt like I was hallucinating or something."

"He had on this little straw hat and a Hawaiian shirt and shorts and sandals. He looked like that guy on the Hawaiian Punch bottle. I almost laughed at him, but I didn't. He had this camera around his neck but it's like ten o'clock at night and pitch black. So he walks up to me and he smiles and says hi and he starts to talk about all the wonderful old buildings in that part of the city. So I said to him you really shouldn't be back here mister and he smiles at me and he says, 'you shouldn't be back here either, child'. In the meantime Jose' is going nutso and telling the guy to get lost but he just keeps on talking about the buildings and stuff. So then the car drives by again, but instead of stopping it just takes off. So then Jose' starts yelling at me and calling me a stupid bitch and that I ruined everything and he started to take a swing at me but the weird guy says 'don't hurt her'. It wasn't like a threat or anything. He just said it in this really soft voice, and then Jose' just stopped and looked at the guy with this like confused look on his face, and then he turned and walked away. So I just started walking and this guy is walking with me and going on and on and I was kind of pissed off because I was going to miss the party. When we got out to Broadway he says to me, can you get home from here? And I say yeah there's a subway stop up the street. So then he says to me, 'you need to be more careful about picking your friends. Just listen to that little voice inside. It will let you know if something is wrong. You need to learn to pay more attention to it'."

"So I'm just staring at this guy and he reaches over and puts his hand on my arm and I start to get that same warm feeling just like before. Then all of a sudden I started to feel really happy and I didn't even care if I missed the stupid party. Then he just says good night and walks away. I found out Jose' got busted later that same night. He was pulled over in a car with some big time dealer and they had like pounds of pot and coke in the trunk and some guns and stuff. Jose' ended up in jail. I think he's still there. I think that was the guy he was waiting for in the alley."

"I guess you were pretty lucky the guy showed up."

"Yeah, but I don't think it was luck. Not any more. I mean there was no reason for that guy to be back in some dark alley in the city, dressed like he was and with an expensive camera around his neck. I mean there's no way he wouldn't be mugged in like ten seconds. It wasn't a place where tourists would ever go."

"Well, I suppose it could have been a coincidence. Maybe he was just lost."

"Maybe, but I don't think so. It was the way he talked to me, like he knew me and was looking out for me. And there was that feeling that came over me."

"And it happened again, after that?"

"Yeah. The night I got roofied."

"You got what?"

"Roofied. Its real name is Rohypnol. It's a date rape drug. Guys drop some in your drink and the next thing you know you're waking up in some strange place feeling sick and hurting from being raped. Some evil bastards get a girl passed out and they shoot them up with heroin and try to get them addicted. Sometimes it kills them."

70

"Were you raped?"

"No. I went to this party to meet some friends and all I can remember is sitting at a table and feeling like I couldn't move. The next thing I remember was waking up on a park bench. I was leaning against this older guy. I didn't recognize him. I was really disoriented and I was so wasted I couldn't talk. He was all dressed up and I was drooling all over his overcoat. I was really embarrassed. The thing is, he was really cool about it. He asked me if I wanted to get a cup of coffee. I was still pretty out of it, and I just said okay. We went to this little all night café. We talked about all sorts of things. He was really smart and it seemed like he understood my life, almost like he had been homeless himself. We talked for an hour or so and then he asked if I would like him to walk me home. I never do that, but that night I did. On the way to where I was staying I asked him how I got to the park. He just said a friend brought me. Later, I asked the people who were with me that night what happened. They just said they lost track of me and thought I went home. That's not unusual for me. I do that sometimes if I don't like the crowd. But I still don't know what happened. None of them knew how I got to the park and I didn't know anybody else at the party."

I looked at her for a moment to see if there was more to the story but she was back inside her head again.

"That is a little unusual," I said, finally. "I'll give you that. You were drugged though. It's not surprising you wouldn't remember everything."

"Yeah, but nobody else remembered anything either. How could somebody take me away in front of my friends, without anybody seeing me? It wasn't a big party. There weren't that many people there."

"Did you ask the guy who he was?"

"No, that's the other really odd thing. Somehow when these things happen, it's like I'm with somebody I know really well. Like an old friend or something. Except I really didn't know him at all. When he left, he shook my hand and it was like I woke up from a dream. I didn't feel drugged anymore. I never think about their names or who they are until after they're gone. Then I'm mad at myself for not asking."

"Well, if you have somebody looking out for you, I have to believe it's a good thing. Whatever the explanation is."

"I guess, but why me? People get into trouble all the time and nobody shows up to help them. The guy in the park said sometimes your life gets out of balance and you need some help to get it straightened out. He said it happens all the time, everyday for lots of people but they just don't notice, or they think it was just a coincidence. I don't know what to think about that. Sometimes I don't understand what my life is all about. I mean, I'm not doing anything useful. All I'm doing is keeping myself alive and trying not to get into trouble. It's like I don't really have a future. It's just the same thing every day. I mean, what's the point anyway? "

"I think we all feel like that sometimes, Megan. Maybe you just think about it more because you don't have as many distractions as most of us."

5

The house in Richmond was a late nineteenth century Victorian surrounded by a white picket fence. It was the kind of place that would have looked uncomfortable in a new coat of paint. Megan asked me if I would mind waiting in the car while she went inside to talk to Annabel's friend. In case she needed a ride to the bus station, she said. She seemed really uncomfortable and I felt sorry for her. She had been in the house for a long time, but I didn't mind waiting. If nothing else, it gave me a chance to try to sort things out a little. More than once on the drive down I had looked over at her and wondered what it felt like to live like she did, but it was too far outside of my experience. I had to admit she was fun to be around. There was a kind of logic to her world view but it was unlike any I had come across before. I guessed surviving on the streets of New York would give anyone a skewed view of reality. I had met a few people from bad circumstances before, and a lot of them tended to embellish their life stories to make up for their deprivations. I didn't think Megan was putting on an act. She seemed to be amazingly grounded in her life and I was intrigued. In a way, I was sorry I wasn't going to be there to see how things turned out for her. It seemed to me she was on the verge of going through a major life change. I hoped it was for the better. I must have dropped off to sleep when I was startled by a tapping on the window. She was standing there looking at me with a curious expression on her face. She was holding a letter in her hand. I lowered the window.

"She wants to talk to you."

"To me? Why?"

"I don't know but she does. Do you mind?"

"Are you going to stay here?"

"I don't know. Maybe."

I walked up to the house feeling like I was entering a dark room. For the first time since I had met Megan I got the feeling I was being drawn into something I would be better off walking away from. Before I could knock, an elderly woman opened the door and motioned for me to come in. She was wearing an ankle-length blue dress with a flower pattern and lace around the collar. She looked to be at least eighty with pure white hair that she had pulled back in a bun. Her eyes were clear and sharp but there was no welcoming smile. She was stooped over at the shoulders so that she had to turn her head a little to look up at me. In another woman it might have seemed a posture of deference but, somehow, I felt like an errant schoolboy being led off to the stool in the corner. She led me to the parlor and indicated for me to sit. The furniture was old but not worn and the room looked comfortable and lived in. I sat down on the couch and she sat in a chair across from me. I had to shift my position to see her around a vase of fresh-cut white roses that were placed on the coffee table between us.

"My name is Rachel. Would you like something to drink dear, a cup of tea perhaps? Or do you need to use the bathroom?"

Her voice crackled with age, but she spoke with a quiet self-assurance that belied her years. She reminded me of a philosophy professor I had known at the university.

"No I'm fine. Megan said you wanted to talk to me?"

She paused for a moment and studied my face.

"Yes," she said finally, "I wanted to find out what your intentions are."

"My intentions? You mean about Megan? I don't have any intentions. I just agreed to drive her down here."

"Why?"

"Why did I help her? I don't know why. She needed help. I have some time, so I gave her a ride. I was going through here anyway. I didn't give it much thought, to tell you the truth."

"You feel something for her?"

"What do you mean by feel something? She's a nice kid. I like her. I've only known her for a couple of days. I'm fifteen years older than she is, for God's sake. Look, if you think I'm trying to take advantage of her you're wrong."

"No, I don't think that, dear, and neither does she."

"Okay, so what do you want to know?"

"I want to know if you are going to finish what you started."

"Finish? I thought that's what I just did."

"Perhaps, but the girl needs you and it would be better for both of you if you saw this through to the end."

"What do you mean to the end? I thought you were going to help her."

"I can give her a place to stay for a while but I am an old woman. I cannot give her the help she really needs right now."

"What does she need?"

"You will have to ask her about that yourself."

"Why, what's the big secret?"

She paused for a few seconds. The house was utterly quiet, except for the soft ticking of a grandfather clock in the foyer. It felt like the reading room in a library. A gray house cat walked in and froze for a moment as it discovered me. It felt like I had stumbled into a different universe.

"The big secret, as you put it dear, is life itself. Why are we here? What is our purpose? How do we choose the right path to take? You strike me as a man who has asked himself such questions and who is perhaps not entirely happy with the answers you have come to."

"What's that got to do with helping Megan?"

"Perhaps nothing. Perhaps everything. It may be that in reality it is she who is helping you."

"Look, I don't mean to insult you, but you're talking in riddles. You don't know anything about me."

"That is true, although Megan has told me a little about you."

"She doesn't know me either."

"Perhaps not, but I think you would be surprised by how fully she has described you to me. It would seem, at this point in time, you are being tested by your life just as Megan is."

"What do you mean?"

"You are in transit, Mark. Not just between locations on a map, but between chapters in your life. Your existence, as you have known it, has come unraveled and something new awaits you. The fabric of that new something will be woven of the remnants you chose to hold on to from your past experience and the threads you create in this time of change. The choices you make in the next few weeks will help determine what the tapestry of your life will look like as you move into the future. It is remarkable, and I believe, not an accident that you and Megan have come together at this time. She did not choose you at random. She told me she stood at the doorway of the restaurant for nearly two hours looking for the right person. She chose you."

"Why me?"

"I don't know the answer to that question. Perhaps not even Megan knows. Some of the choices we make in this life come from deep places in the heart, beyond our conscious minds. Megan is quite attuned to her deeper self. She has learned to rely on it when a decision must be made. Megan understands the journey of the soul and she has embraced it. You look at her and see a young woman suffering deprivation but I think you see something else as well. Something you cannot quite grasp. It draws you to her and it has inspired you to offer her your help, at least up to this point. Although it is true you have reached out to help Megan, the equally important reality is that she has reached out to help you move forward. Your futures are bound together, at least for now. How long that is true and to what end you will only know as events unfold."

"So why didn't she choose someone more her own age?"

"I suppose because she is not looking for a mate. She has put those considerations aside for now. She likes you though. She feels safe with you and I think she senses you are a decent man. One capable of understanding what she is going through. Also, she is worried about you."

"How do you know that?"

"I don't know. This is what she told me. I asked her why she chose you and do you know what she said?"

"No."

"She said it was because you are alone like she is, and your soul is crying."

"I just shook my head. "I don't even know what that means."

"Just that you are in pain and she can see that you are and she wants to help you."

I was completely thrown off balance and didn't know how to respond. I think down deep I had already come to suspect there was more to my encounter with Megan than just giving her a ride. Still, to get more involved with her life was a leap into the unknown and I was afraid of what it might lead to. At the same time, another voice was telling me this was important. If I were ever going to change my life it was going to start here and if I walked away I was condemning myself to repeating the same existence all over again. Safe and secure and empty. I felt like a door had opened up in front of me and it was time to walk through.

"Look, I wouldn't mind helping Megan, but I need to know what I'm getting into. It sounds like you're asking me to make some kind of open ended commitment here. I need to know what's going on. I don't want to be put into a position where I'm forced to do something I don't want to do."

"You will not be forced to do anything."

"I don't mean physically forced. I mean I don't want Megan to start depending on me and then at some point have to walk away."

"I understand your concern, and it speaks well of you. It tells me you do care for the girl and she is in good hands. I'll tell you what I know. Megan has been given a gift by Annabel Weiss, a dear friend of mine from New York City. It is a very valuable book that has been missing for quite some time. There is a man in Charleston who has researched the book and believes he may have located it. He is an art dealer and he has contacted Annabel to see if she is interested in selling it. Annabel has no family and the few remaining friends she has are very old. She has developed a great love for Megan and she wants to help her start a new life."

"Why didn't Annabel just give Megan this guy's information herself? Why send her to see you?"

"She wanted me to meet Megan so we could discuss her situation. Perhaps to see if I agreed with her about whom Megan is. Also, I must tell you that Annabel is a little frightened. She is aware that others know about this book and want it for themselves. She believes someone is watching her. Her first concern was to get Megan out of the city as soon as possible so that no harm would come to her. That is all I really know. The man Megan will be meeting in Charleston knows more about the book. Annabel was also very concerned that Megan might be taken advantage of in these negotiations. She is not experienced in such things. Annabel is a woman of deep faith and she believed in her heart that someone would come forward to help Megan in this time of need. It appears that someone is you. I think Megan made the right choice."

"I don't know. I don't know if I want to make this kind of commitment."

"I understand your dilemma. Really, I do. But if you do want to help her, why don't you just at least agree to go with her to meet this man in Charleston? If you are going to Florida anyway it would be on the way. You can perhaps advise her as to how to proceed from that point, after she understands what is involved. After that you can just get on with your journey if that is what you wish to do."

Megan was leafing through a magazine when I got back to the car and she didn't look up at me. I climbed into the driver's seat and just sat there with my hands on the wheel, staring out the windshield. I was still trying to figure out what had just happened.

"You don't have to do this." She said, finally.

"You know what she said to me?"

"No, but I know she thinks you should help me, but you don't have to, really. I can take care of myself. I know you have other plans. If you could just drop me off at a bus station, I'd really appreciate it."

I looked over at her.

"She told me you have to meet someone in Charleston."

"Yeah. That thing that Annabel gave me is some kind of a book. Rachel doesn't have it. I have to find it."

"It sounds like some kind of game."

"No, it's just lost and I have to find it if I want it."

"And she didn't tell you anything about it?"

"No. She gave be the name and phone number of this guy in Charleston. She said he would tell me all about it and help me figure out how to find it. Look, you really don't have to do anything else. I appreciate you bringing me this far. I can manage from here."

We sat there in silence again. I really didn't know what to do but the more I listened to Megan the more I realized how much she needed help and how vulnerable she was, even just as a young woman out on her own with not much money and without any friends. I looked over at her again, but she wouldn't look back at me. I started the engine.

"Well if you're going to be traveling with me you're going to need some decent clothes."

"What's wrong with these?" She asked, smiling.

"Well, at least a new coat. One that fits you. And a decent pair of shoes and some jeans that still have the knees in them. And while you're at it you need to get rid of that backpack and get a suitcase. I saw a shopping center on the way here. I want to get a road atlas anyway."

"I think I should save my money for traveling expenses."

"Save your money for when you get to wherever you're going. This is on me."

"You don't have to do that. Really. I want to pay."

"I'll tell you what. You can pay me by telling me some more of your stories and let me pick out a couple of your drawings. Deal?"

"Deal." She said. She turned away as if she was interested in something outside her window, but I could see she was smiling and it made me feel good inside."

"Do you have an appointment with this man you're meeting in Charleston? Is he expecting you?"

"He's expecting me, but Rachel didn't say when. I think it's up to me."

"Okay. So we're going to have to swing by my friends place on the way. We may have to spend the night there. Do you think that'll be all right?"

"Sure. I don't think it matters. Rachel didn't know when I was coming anyway so I'm sure the guy in Charleston doesn't know either. How long are you going to stay at your friend's house?"

"We didn't really make any firm plans because I wasn't sure of the timing. I thought I'd stop in on the way down to Florida and then make arrangements to come back in a week or two. Whenever he can manage some time off."

"Will they mind? That I'm with you I mean. You could drop me off somewhere and I could wait for you."

"Of course they won't mind. Why would they?"

"I don't know. Maybe they wouldn't want a homeless person in their house."

"First of all they aren't like that. And second, if they were I wouldn't want to go visit them anyway. And third you need to stop thinking of yourself like that. You are just as good as anybody else and from what I've seen, better than a lot of people. You don't have to be embarrassed about your life."

"I'm not. I just thought you might be."

"I'm not like that either, Megan. I'll be happy to have you with me."

6

Megan seemed like a different person. It was as if the weight of all her doubts and fears had been lifted and she was suddenly free. She busied herself removing tags from the clothing she had bought and folding them neatly in her new overnight bag. She was like a little kid at Christmas. I95 through the southern states is like driving through a green tunnel. There's not much to see except dirt roads and pine trees and the occasional fireworks stand and billboards for 'South of the Border'. We crossed into North Carolina and the speed limit bumped up to seventy. When she finished arranging her things she looked over and smiled at me.

"Are you all done?" I asked.

"Yeah. Thanks again for the clothes. I really needed them."

"So are you going to tell me what's in the letter?   I mean it would help me to know what I've gotten myself into here."

"Do you want me to read it to you? I mean it really doesn't say anything about how I am supposed to find this thing."

"Sure, I'd like to hear it."

She opened the envelope and removed the two hand-written pages.   She looked at them again as if she wanted to make sure nothing had changed.

"Okay,   here   goes.   But   it's   a   little embarrassing."

Dear Megan:

I cannot begin to tell you how much it has meant to me to find you and to see what a lovely young woman you are. For many years, since my mother died, I have felt removed. Not only from the world but from my past. I loved your mother when she was a little girl. I almost feel like she was the younger sister I never had. I lost touch with her over the years, as I have with almost all of my old friends. You have awakened many beautiful old memories for me and I am so grateful. I am especially grateful for your wonderful generosity, in returning my necklace to me. I know you loved it almost as much as I do and that it was hard for you to let it go. It has meant so much to me to have it at this time in my life. Thank you.

It was painful to hear of the difficult existence you have been living and yet I think your life has served to bring out the best in you. You are remarkably strong and your heart sees deeply into things. You see the world for what it is, without all the nonsense that distracts us as we wonder through our days. I know that life will not be able to change you now, no matter what happens, and that you will find a way to use your gift to help those you meet during your journey home. I hope you find great love and happiness along the way.

There is something I want you to have. It is a lovely book that was purchased by my father before he died. My mother showed it to me once a very long time ago and it was the most beautiful thing I have ever seen. I wish I could just wrap it up and give it to you but I can't for reasons you will learn in due time. I suppose it is true that all things of great beauty require great effort. I thought this book was lost forever, until I received word from an art *dealer in Charleston, South Carolina that records of its continued existence have been found. Rachel will tell you how to get in touch with this man and I am hopeful that he will be* able to help you find it. I *have promised to pay him a commission if he is successful, but the book belongs to you and you alone. I hope you will remember me and pray for me. May God bless you and keep you safe.*

Love always, Annabel.

"Well that's a really nice letter, Megan. Sounds like you made quite an impression on her."

"Oh, I don't know. I think she would have liked anybody who was kind to her. I think she's one of the loneliest people I've ever met. I'm glad I could cheer her up a little. I really like her."

"I wonder why she didn't give you the letter herself."

"I don't know. Maybe she didn't want me to read it while she was there. Rachel said it was because she really wanted me to get out of the city. I don't know what she thought was going to happen, but I'm glad I'm out of there now. Thanks again for helping me."

"I don't mind. I like a good mystery anyway. I'll take you down to Charleston at least and if you want me to, I'll come with you to meet this art dealer. After that we'll just see how it goes."

"That would be really nice of you. I was worried about meeting this guy. I don't know anything about him."

"No problem. Now how about another one of your stories."

She didn't say anything for a few moments and when I looked over at her she was biting the corner of her lip and looking down at her feet.

"What?"

"I don't know. I'm not sure if I should tell you this or not."

"Why?"

"Well, it's not really a funny story. It's something that really happened and it's a little strange."

"That's all right. I'm getting used to it."

"Okay. I know I've told you some weird stuff but I don't want you to start thinking I'm some kind of wacko or something, because I'm not."

"I know you're not. In fact I'm beginning to think you could be the least crazy person I've ever met."

"Really?"

"No."

She laughed. "Okay then, but don't say I didn't warn you. So this one morning I was out by Columbus Circle. It must have been around 9:30 or 10:00 because most of the commuters were gone and it was pretty quiet for a change. So I'm walking through the plaza. I can't even remember where I was going, but I looked over and there's this guy standing in the fountain, like in between the streams that shoot up into the air. The water isn't deep or anything but the thing is, this guy was wearing a suit and tie and he was holding a briefcase. At first I thought he was being photographed, like it was some kind of a riff on a Rene Magritte painting. Have you seen any of his? The businessmen in the suits and bowler hats and the apples?"

"Sure."

"Anyway there wasn't a photographer anywhere I could see. This guy didn't have his pants rolled up or anything. He was just standing there with his shoes and socks on and his pant legs in the water. People were walking by and I guess most of them didn't even notice. I don't know if they did or not because that's the way it is in New York. If people don't want to deal with something, they just pretend they don't see it. Actually, I think that's what they do in the beginning but after a while I think they really don't see things they don't want to see. You know what I mean? It's like they see things with their eyes but somehow it never gets through to their brains. I think that changes people after a while. I think their world starts to shrink until they're living in a little box and they're trapped inside. I think that's why people in New York seem so rude. They've tuned people out so much that they aren't even real to them any more. They're just part of the scenery like a lamp post or a no parking sign. Some 'thing' that they have to deal with. Now everybody walks around staring at their phone. They're just gone from the world. I never want to live that way."

She looked over at me to see if I was still listening.

"Yeah, I know what you mean." I said. "It isn't just in New York. It's that way in most big cities I've been in."

She nodded. "It isn't just in big cities, either, it's everywhere. So now there's this other thing they call the World Wide Web and it's so ironic because that's exactly what it is. Like a huge spider web and everyone is trapped in it like a bunch of flies. It captures you and sucks the life out of you. The whole world has gone crazy. Now people say they have an on-line presence. That's where they live. In the real world they're just empty shells."

I didn't know how to respond, so I just nodded my head.

"So anyway I stood there looking at this man for a few minutes and finally I yelled over to him. I said. 'Hey are you all right?' but he didn't answer. I don't know if he didn't hear me or if he was just ignoring me or if he heard my voice but somehow didn't understand the words. There are a lot of people who just lose it in the city. I mean, some of it's drugs and alcohol but some people seem to just be going along with their lives and then suddenly they find themselves in a place that they don't recognize any more. That has to be really frightening. Some of them just become homeless and they walk around muttering to themselves. As long as they don't cause any problems nobody bothers with them. I've met quite a few. Some are actually really nice people. They just have a different way of looking at things. Of course, some of them end up doing something bizarre or violent and the cops come and cart them off to Belleview. Nobody should ever have to go to that place."

She paused and took a sip of her water.

"Anyway, I know a lot of artists in the city. Most of them seem a little odd to people on the outside. A lot of them are Bi-polar. I read once that most of the really great writers and artists in history have been Bi-polar or at least suffering from off and on depression. They didn't have medicine for it when Van Gogh cut his ear off. Unless maybe Absinthe, but that just whacks you out. Now they can treat it, but the medicine makes you flat-line. You can't feel anything anymore, so it keeps you from doing anything creative. Most of the artists I know won't take the stuff. So sometimes when you see them they're exploding with energy and other times they're off somewhere crying their eyes out. People don't understand what they're going through. They just write them off. Sometimes they just can't take it any more and they check out. Some just become odd."

"I know this one artist named Leon who has conversations with the horses that pull the carriages over in central park. He knows all of them and he has these long conversations with them. I mean lots of people talk to the horses but they apparently talk back to Leon. It sounds strange, I know, but if you watch them for a while, you would swear they were having a conversation with him. They nod their heads and stamp their hooves and sometimes they seem pissed off and sometimes it even looks like they're laughing. Everybody thinks he's a nutcase but how does anyone really know. How can anyone say the horses aren't communicating with him? I mean it seems to me reality is just some kind of unspoken agreement we have with each other. Like everyone agrees that there is a color we call red but how do we know everyone is seeing the same thing we call red. I had an art teacher once who said some people can see hundreds of shades of a color and some people can't see it at all. But that's really not a good example because it's really some actual physical difference in a person's brain."

"The thing is, I took LSD a few times, and it really freaked me out. I wouldn't take it again.

It's way too scary. It's like being in a dream only you don't know what's real and what isn't and you can't wake up. Think about that for a minute. It's kind of cool at first but after a while you just want it to stop. At least I did. It really sucks and it goes on for hours. They say some people think they can fly and they jump off of buildings and stuff. I never saw anything like that happen."

"Anyway this one time I was with this girl named Amber. She was one of those people who have like a zillion freckles all over her face and her body and they really made her skin look amber colored. I used to wonder if her parents named her after they saw what she looked like when she was first born. I don't know if you're born with all those freckles or they come later. So anyway, Amber and I were in this coffee house over in the Village and I was sitting across from her and we were both tripping our asses off. I was looking at her and all of a sudden the freckles came off her face and just sort of hovered in front of her like a swarm of little bees or something. And I sort of leaned over to the side and I looked around this ball of little bees that were her freckles and I saw her face with no freckles on it. It was like I was seeing her real face for the first time. In a way it was really cool, but it made me wonder what it says about

99

reality, you know? I mean, I know I was tripping and my perception was out of whack, but still I saw what I saw."

"So how does anyone really know what we're seeing is real or if it's just some kind of a projection? How do we know anything is real at all? Maybe we are all just asleep somewhere and we're sharing the same dream. We're sharing this dream and the dream is the world. And maybe when the world is going through tough times it's because we are all having the same bad dream. Like during the depression when the President, I can't remember his name, but he said 'The only thing we have to fear is fear itself'. Or during the Second World War when all of these countries like Germany and Japan and Italy all went crazy together and wanted to burn down the world. Sometimes I think all the bad things in the world are there because of fear. Maybe fear is some kind of magnet that attracts bad stuff to us. I know when I've been afraid a few times some scary things have happened, but I don't know if I was scared because some dangerous things were happening around me or if just being scared made the dangerous things happen by themselves. I think that's how I was able to live for so long in the city without anything bad happening to me, because I wasn't really scared that much. Like when that guy Chuck attacked me. I mean maybe it happened because of what Annabel told me. Maybe it happened because I was a little afraid after I talked to her and if I hadn't maybe nothing would have happened at all. I don't know. Like maybe we are all creating our own reality minute to minute. And then there were those times when those men showed up and helped me when I was out on the edge. It's really confusing."

She paused again and took a deep breath. I didn't say anything, not wanting to interrupt her stream of consciousness. I was becoming more and more amazed by her life, and I had come to understand the rhythm of the telling of it. I knew she would get to the point eventually and sometimes the journey to the point of the story was more interesting than the point itself.

"So anyway I kept asking the guy in the fountain if he was okay but he still didn't answer, so I thought 'what the hell' and I took my sandals off and walked out into the fountain. I walked up to him and I looked him right in the eyes and I just said 'Hi'. His eyes were kind of glazed over but then they started to clear like you know how some lizards have a second transparent eyelid kind of thing. Finally, he looked at me and he said hello. And then he looked down at the water and he said 'Oh look, someone must have left the tub running'. So he starts shouting 'Marie, Marie turn off the faucet' and at that point I didn't know what to do so I told him we should really go find a plumber."

She chuckled. "Anyway, I really wanted to get him out of the fountain because I didn't want the cops to come and take him away. And while I was talking to him these two guys I know came by, Steve and Pauley and they saw me in the fountain so they took off their shoes and they walked out into the fountain too. So now there are four of us standing in the fountain like it's just a normal thing to do, except this guy has a business suit on. So I tell Steve and Pauley what's going on and they each took the guy by the arm and we all just walked out of the fountain. I told him we were going to find Marie. Once we got into the plaza he looked down at his feet and he seemed really confused and he starts having a conversation with someone who wasn't there. Something about defective components in the production stream or something like that. Then all of a sudden he looks out at the street and he starts running and we're like trying to keep up with him. When he gets to the curb he puts his arm out and a cab pulls over. So then the guy just opens the door and gets into the back seat. And he starts to close the door but he stops for a second and he looks up at me and he says, 'I love you. I'll call you when I get back home.'"

She went silent again. I wasn't sure if was the end of the story.

"I wonder what happened to him?" I said, after a few moments.

"Well that's just it. I mean it seemed to me he was in a few different realities all at the same time. Obviously the one where it seemed okay to be standing in the fountain with his shoes and a suit on was wacky. And the one where he was talking to his wife too. But when he got into the cab I wasn't really sure if he was back to his normal reality or if he was just off on some other delusion. Maybe he just had this one little dose of crazy and then he was okay, like he snapped for a second but then it all came back to him. Or maybe he just slips in and out of what we call normal reality all the time. For all I know he could be standing in another fountain somewhere. I'll never know, but what does it mean anyway? If I hadn't walked out into the fountain what would have happened to the guy? I mean maybe he'd be locked up right now in a padded room. Or maybe what I did changed his reality completely. There's no way to know. Maybe I shouldn't have done anything at all. I mean, I thought I was helping him but maybe what I did was the worst thing anyone could have done to him at that moment. After he was gone I looked at his footprints leading our of the fountain and then disappearing at the curb and I thought maybe that was all that was left of his sanity. Like he walked off into oblivion."

"I don't think there's any way to know that, Megan. I think you just have to try to make the right choice. That's what you did. I don't think that can ever be the wrong thing to do, even if it doesn't work out so well for the person you're helping. At least you tried. I think most people wouldn't have cared at all. Maybe that's what he really needed anyway. Somebody from the real world to get him back on track. Just one person who gave a damn."

7

It had been a while since I visited with Walt and Jennifer. Some of Durham looked familiar, but I had to drive around for a while until I found a landmark. The house was on a wide boulevard lined with old-growth hickory trees that had just started to bud after the long winter. The houses were all large, and on beautifully landscaped lots. They were built in a variety of styles, each of them distinct. It looked like a postcard rendition of the American dream. Not a blade of grass was out of place. Megan sat staring out the window with a look on her face like she was about to enter an enemy encampment. Some young boys were kicking a soccer ball around in the front yard. I recognized one of them. His name was Josh, although it seemed like he had grown twice as tall as I remembered him. I shut off the engine and looked over at Megan.

"Well this is the place. What do you think?"

"I've seen places like this before, when we lived in Georgia. I've never been in one though. I used to pretend they were really just fake fronts, like on a movie set."

"Well, they're real enough."

"Yeah, I know. It's just the people inside who have the fake fronts."

"Yeah and they probably have a barbeque grill out back too. Listen, Walt and Jennifer are really very good people. If you had known Walt when he was your age, you would have wanted to hang out with him."

"Why do you say that?"

"Because he shared a lot of your attitudes about society back then. About greed and injustice. About the soulless corporations and the harm they do."

"Did you?"

"Yeah, but I just was never very political. I was too busy trying to get through college. It seemed to come easier for him."

"Looks like he sold out in the end, though."

"We'll see how you feel about that ten years from now. Anyway, try not to be too hard on them."

She smiled at me. "You don't need to worry about me. I'm not a hater or anything like that. I'll try to keep my opinions to myself, as long as they don't back me into a corner."

Jennifer met us at the door. She was tall and slender with long dark hair and just a little gray showing at the part. She had the deepest brown eyes I had ever seen and for a moment I felt that familiar twinge of old memories and young love lost. She gave me a warm hug and then smiled at Megan.

"Hello Jen. This is Megan."

Jennifer hesitated for a moment, waiting perhaps for some hint of a relationship, but then quickly smiled and extended her hand.

"Hi, Megan. Please come in." She looked at the boys and then shouted over at them.

"Josh. Take the game around back. You know you aren't supposed to play ball out here."

Megan gave me a look as we went inside, but she didn't say anything. Jennifer asked us to sit and then went into the kitchen to get some iced tea. The house was beautifully decorated in an American Traditional style. Megan walked around the room looking at the paintings.

"Your friends have good taste. I'll give them that. I like that they didn't pick the paintings to match the furniture."

After a while, we heard a door slam and in a moment a young girl appeared. She was like a smaller version of her mother, with the same willowy build and long dark hair. She was holding a doll and smiling bashfully at Megan.

"Hi, what's your name?" Megan asked.

"I'm Allyson." She said with just the hint of a southern drawl in her voice.

"And what's your doll's name?"

"She's Molly. I was swinging her on the swings. Do you like to swing?"

"I love to swing."

"Do you want to swing me?"

"Megan looked over at me and I nodded."

"Sure, Allyson. I can swing you for a while."

Jennifer came back into the living room and put the drinks down on the coffee table.

"Megan and Alyson found each other. They went out back to swing."

She smiled and nodded her head. "It's so good to see you, Mark. It's been such a long time."

"It's been way too long. I always wished you and Walt had lived a little closer to us."

"How are you holding up? I wish we'd been able to go to the funeral but it was just too far for us to travel with the kids in school and all."

"I'm doing okay. Thank you for the card and the flowers. It helped, hearing from you. The first few months were pretty bad but it's been almost a year now and it's a little easier to deal with. Anyway, your kids look great. I saw Josh out front. He was just a little guy the last time I saw him."

"Yeah, they're really good kids. They grow up so fast it just seems like a blur sometimes. But tell me about Megan. She's really cute. She seems a little young for you though."

I laughed. "You always had a way of getting right to the point. It's not what you think. I'm just giving her a ride down to Charleston. I don't really know her very well."

"Well she seems to like you, anyway."

"Yeah? Go figure."

"Oh come on. You know what I mean. How do you know her?"

"Actually, I met her at a rest stop on the New Jersey turnpike."

"Really? Wow, that doesn't sound like you."

"I guess you're right. Maybe that's the new me. Anyway she's a nice kid. You won't have to hide your silverware."

"What a relief!"

"So what time does Walt get home from work?"

"Walt isn't here Mark. He left."

"When will he be back?"

"I don't know. He left almost a month ago."

"You mean he moved out? Oh my god. I'm really sorry, Jennifer, I didn't know. What happened?"

"No. We didn't split up or anything. At least, I don't think that's what's going on. To tell you the truth I don't really have a clue what happened. I just know he started getting strange. Distant, I guess. First with me and then with the kids. Then he just left. The kids are taking it pretty bad. Especially Josh. I told them their dad had to go away for business but they want to know when he's coming home. I don't know what to tell them. I'm sorry. I should have told you when you called. I hope I'm not putting you out. I was hoping he would be back by now. He was really looking forward to seeing you. "

"Where is he?"

"Well, like I said, he's been gone for almost a month. I didn't even know where he went until about a week ago. He's in Key Largo. Or at least he was last week."

"He just took off?"

111

She took a tissue from her pocket and dabbed at her eyes.

"He's in some kind of trouble, Mark. I don't know what he got himself into but I know he's afraid. He told me he had to leave for a little while because it would be better for me and the kids if he wasn't around. He said it wouldn't be long but he won't tell me what's wrong. I'm really scared. I think he's having to deal with some people he doesn't trust. It's so out of character for him. I mean, you know Walt as well as anyone. He's never lacked for confidence but he always seemed to know how far to take things. Whatever is going on, I think he got himself in over his head."

"Did you talk to anyone about it?"

"I don't know who to talk to. I tried to get a hold of somebody at the company but they won't tell me anything. They just said he's on assignment. I thought about going to the police but I'm afraid that may just make things worse. He's been calling me all along and he sends money every week so it's not a missing person issue."

"Is he still working? I mean, how is he getting the money to send to you?"

"I don't know. He's still employed as far as I know. I don't understand how he can be working and not be there at his office. He never had to travel much before and never for this length of time."

"Is he still with Oracle?"

"No, no. He left them almost a year ago. It was right around the time of Ann's funeral. I guess it's been a while since you two talked. He got involved in a start-up with one of his old managers."

"Doing what?"

"I'm not really sure. It has something to do with software. Computer stuff. Apparently it's some secret project. I've never really understood his work. He tried to explain it to me a few times but I guess my eyes just glaze over. You know me. If it isn't something to do with the arts, anything too technical. All I know is he was making good money and he seemed to be pretty happy doing whatever it was. Then, all of a sudden, he took off."

"And he didn't give you any hint of what's going on?"

"No. Actually, I was hoping he might have said something to you."

"I haven't spoken to Walt since the funeral, and we didn't really get into anything about his life, other than he said you and the kids were doing well. I assumed he was still with Oracle. I wasn't thinking very well at the time. We were supposed to talk after it all settled out, but I guess I haven't really been up to being sociable."

"I'm really sorry Mark. I don't mean to be bothering you with my problems, especially now. I can't imagine what you've been going through."

"No. It's okay, really. I've pretty much worked through it all anyway. All except the part about what I'm going to do next. Do you think it would help if I talked to him?"

"Maybe. He always said you were the only real friend he ever had. But I don't want to bother you with this. Anyway, I don't have a phone number for him. His cell number just rolls over to voice mail and when I call the number he's dialing from, it just rings. Nobody picks up."

"I'm sorry to ask this Jennifer, but do you think it could be another woman?"

"It's okay. At first I thought the same thing, but I don't really think so. I know there was a young analyst at work that he liked. He talked about her sometimes, but I never thought there was anything to it really. Just work friends, you know. I think I would know if it were something like that and besides we were getting along fine. I mean there were arguments, like there are in every marriage. There's something else going on. I don't know what to do."

"Has anyone else called and asked for him. Anyone you don't know?"

"I got some calls a couple of weeks ago but that's not unusual. He had been working with some head-hunters before he left. I got the feeling he was a little worried about the company. I just assumed it was about a new position."

"And nobody stopped by to ask for him?"

"No. I did see a car parked down the street a few times, that I didn't recognize. It was one of those ridiculous, gigantic SUVs. A Cadillac or Lincoln or something. You couldn't help but notice it. There were two men wearing suits, but they never tried to talk to me. They never came to the house. I just assumed they were Real Estate agents."

"I think you should try his company again. They have to tell you something?"

"Actually, I don't think they have to tell me anything. I mean if I told them I thought he was in some kind of trouble they might have to speak to me or to a lawyer at least. I don't know. Anyway, they have to know he left. I don't want to make things worse."

"Well, I'd be glad to talk to him if it would help. Why don't you take my cell phone number and the next time he calls, ask him to call me. I should be down in the Miami area in a day or two. If you can find out where he's staying, maybe I can go talk to him."

"Thanks Mark. I'd really be grateful. Now, you and Megan have to stay for dinner. The kids would be happy for the company and so would I. I'm not the greatest cook in the world but we have plenty."

"Sure. That would be great."

"It's really is so good to see you again. Do you have a place to stay tonight?"

"We'll just stop at one of the hotels out by the highway. This time of year it won't be a problem."

"Don't do that. I have a spare bedroom and there's a fold out sofa in the family room. I'd like you both to stay the night. Please."

"I don't want to make a lot of work for you."

"It's no work at all. Aside from all the worry, I've been really lonely and I can't really talk to anyone about it. I feel so much better just talking with you. You would really be doing me a big favor if you stayed over."

After dinner Megan helped Jennifer and Allyson in the kitchen. I spent some time with Josh, watching him play a video game. We didn't talk about his dad but I could see the he was glad for the company. Allyson would not go to bed until Megan promised to read her a story. Once the kids had settled down we all moved out to the family room and Jennifer opened a bottle of wine. We made small talk for a while and Jennifer was obviously curious about Megan. She couldn't resist the urge to dig into her life a little. Megan looked a little uncomfortable and I tried to steer the conversation toward some safer ground. It didn't work.

"So what do you do in New York, Megan?"

"You mean for money? I draw caricatures of people."

"That sounds interesting."

"Yeah. It's fun sometimes. At least when the weather's nice."

"Well you must do pretty well with it. I've heard it's an expensive place to live."

"Yeah. Well that depends. I didn't have my own place to live in, so I didn't have to pay any rent."

Jennifer looked at me briefly and then turned back to Megan.

"I'm sorry Megan. I didn't mean to pry."

Megan shrugged her shoulders. "It's okay. I'm not ashamed of it or anything."

"No. Of course not. Hey, maybe you could do a couple of drawings for the kids. I'll bet they'd love it. I mean, I'll pay for them, of course."

"Sure. But you can't pay me. I don't charge my friends. You made us a nice dinner and we're staying here tonight so that's enough."

"Megan is being modest." I said. "She is a terrific artist. Show her the drawing you did of me on the way down, Megan."

"It's up in my suitcase. I'll show it to you before I go. Anyway, this is a really nice house. I like the paintings in your living room. Who did them?"

"Actually they are all local artists. There are a couple of good galleries in town. Two of them are by students at the University. Do you do any painting?"

"Not really. I did a few when I was taking classes but I don't have anyplace to work right now. Anyway, I like to draw mostly. So, did the paintings cost a lot?"

"No. That's the advantage of buying local artists. You can get some of their work before they get discovered."

"So you buy them because they might be worth a lot of money some day?"

I glanced over at her, hoping to keep her from getting into something confrontational, but she was not to be dissuaded. Jennifer paused for a moment before answering. I think she knew she was being baited but she was gracious in her response. She smiled at Megan.

"I really don't care how much money they're worth, Megan. I like them for what they are. It's just that, once an artist gets well known it's nearly impossible to get anything original at a reasonable price. It's what they're worth to me that I care about. I'd rather have an original that I really like by an unknown artist than a copy of a masterpiece."

Megan smiled and nodded. "Yeah, that's how I feel about it too."

There was a bit of an uncomfortable silence then. Finally Jennifer turned to me.

"So have you given any thought about what you're going to do now, Mark? I mean, I'm sure you've thought about it, but any ideas yet?"

"I've been thinking about it a lot but I haven't really come to any decisions. That's what this trip is about really. I thought a change in location would help me give it all a fresh look."

"Do you think you'll stay in Vermont?"

"Actually, I don't think so. I like New England, but it reminds me too much of my past and I'm trying to let go of that."

"Sure. I can understand that. Any ideas where then?"

"Not really. I guess it depends on what I decide to do for a living."

"You should look for something down in this area. There are a lot of good companies and the weather's great."

"I actually thought about that. We'll see."

In a while, Megan asked if we would mind if she turned in. Jen took her up to the guest room and got her settled. When she came back down she refilled our glasses. We talked late into the evening about old times. I hadn't had that kind of conversation for a long time and not for years with Jennifer. It made me wonder why we hadn't made a go of it. She was really stressed out about her situation but as the time ticked by and a new bottle was opened, she began to relax.

"So I don't mean to pry and if you don't want to talk about it we don't have to, but what happened between you and Ann? I mean, what made you want to separate. It seemed like you two had a great thing going. Really, I always envied the two of you. I guess because you didn't start a family. You seemed to be there just for each other."

"Well we couldn't. I don't know if you and Ann ever talked about it, but she wasn't able to get pregnant."

"We did talk about it. I felt really bad for her when she told me."

"The marriage counselor seemed to think that was part of the problem. Not so much that we didn't have children but that somehow that choice had been taken away from us. I guess there was some resentment. Not with one another, but with life in general. I suppose a lot of it was my fault. I've never been the most exciting guy in the room. Nothing has ever come that easy for me. I just learned to keep my head down and plod away at it. Not very inspiring I guess, but that's what worked for me. Anyway, you know how it is with relationships. You get used to one another. The little things that annoy you become magnified. The glamour starts to go out of it when it grinds down to living every day. That's when that other thing is supposed to kick in. That love you develop that's unselfish and kind. I think we had that for a while. At least we were moving that way. For some reason we couldn't hold on to it. I really don't know why. Looking back, I think she was trying to tell me it wasn't working for her but I wasn't paying attention. Maybe it would have been different if we had kids. I don't know. You would have to tell me."

"I think it does that, but it can be overwhelming too. They take up your whole life. I mean, don't get me wrong, I couldn't love my kids more than I already do, and I love being a mom. Sometimes I think if Walt and I could just take a month off and go to an island without them, we could maybe get some of that feeling back again. You know. Get some perspective back. Lately, with whatever Walt is into with his job, it hardly feels like there's anything left between us. He's been so strange. It seems almost like someone else is occupying his body. When we make love it feels like he's just angry with me. Almost like he's trying to hurt me. I don't believe he really wants that. Not really. It just seems like he's conflicted some how. Like there's something eating at him inside."

I didn't know how to respond. I think Jen realized she had stepped into uncomfortable territory and she quickly changed the subject.

"So what made you decide to sell your business?"

"I don't know. I think it was just time. In the beginning it was exciting, building something like that. Making it grow. After ten years it was humming along pretty well but it started to get more difficult. Most of what we did could be done cheaper in Asia. A lot of businesses like ours went under. We were still doing pretty well but the writing was on the wall. Someone made us an offer. At first I was reluctant but in the end it seemed like the best thing to do. Especially after Ann passed away."

"That's a lot of change all at once. How in the world have you been keeping it all together?"

"I've had my moments, believe me. There have been nights when I woke up in a dead panic, for no reason I was conscious of. A lot of days I felt like I was just sleepwalking through it all. I really had lost my ability to concentrate on anything. I guess that's why I decided to hit the road. I just needed to make a clean break of it."

"That's a hard thing to handle alone. Was there anyone you could talk to about it?"

"Not really. Not anyone I felt close enough to."

"I wish you had come down to see us. I feel guilty for not making more of an effort."

"Thanks but you shouldn't feel like that. In the end, no matter how much people want to help, you have to make the hard choices alone. Not that I wouldn't have enjoyed the company."

"And now that you're here, we're a total mess. Life can really pull the rug out from under you, can't it?"

"Yeah, well you should hear what Megan has been going through. I'm amazed she's still alive."

"What happened to her?"

"She's one of those people who just fell through the cracks. She was living a tenuous existence to begin with and then her mother died and left her with nothing. She is really a remarkable young woman though. There is an uncommon strength in her and she has a warm heart."

"Why is she going to Charleston?"

"Someone she knows in the city gave her a rare book. She's going to meet an art dealer to find out about it. I'm hoping it will help her find a better life. We'll see."

"I hope it works out for her. And for you too."

By the end of the evening we were both laughing like we had back when we were young and still at arms length from the troubles of the world. Finally we had to call it a night. She helped me pull out the sleep sofa and brought me some sheets and a blanket. She kissed me goodnight. I could taste the wine on her lips and the pressure of her body against me wakened part of me that had been dormant for a long time. It turned into something more that it was meant to be. I don't know who pulled away first. I just know it was hard for me to let her go.

8

We arrived in Charleston late in the afternoon. I decided to treat Megan to a nice hotel and chose the Mills House downtown. She looked stunned.

"Wow, what a dump!" She said, stifling a laugh."

"Yeah, it's a little step up from the Days Inn."

"Are we going to stay here tonight? Really?"

"Yeah, unless it doesn't suit you."

"I'll hold my nose and put up with it."

We took the elevator up to the third floor and found the room halfway down the corridor. Megan immediately checked out the bathroom and then opened the bedroom closet. She opened the sliding door and stepped out onto the balcony, leaning her arms on the railing for a while and looking out at the old town. I watched her and I had to smile. She seemed almost giddy and I thought this could very well be the first time in her life she was ever in a decent hotel room. A horse-drawn carriage went by beneath the window and she waved to the driver. In a while she turned and came back into the room. She opened all of the dresser drawers and then went for the hall closet.

"Wow there's even an iron and an ironing board in here. There're two bathrobes too, are they for us."

"Not permanently."

She opened the mini-bar and took a soda and a bag of peanuts.

"Is this okay?" She asked.

"Sure, but don't ruin your dinner."

She plopped down on the bed and rolled over on her elbows. Staring up at me.

"What do you think we should do first?"

"It's up to you. If you want, we can call the number Rachel gave you. Maybe we can meet this guy tonight."

"Do you mind calling? I don't know what to say."

I dialed the number and it rang for a long time. I was about to hang up when a man answered. I explained who I was and asked when we could meet. The man, whose name was Hamilton Biers, suggested we meet for dinner. He recommended a little Italian restaurant on Church Street and I agreed on eight o'clock.

It was a cozy little place down the street from the old slave market. Every table was lighted by a candle in an ancient looking, straw-wrapped Chianti bottle. The only other illumination came from the miniature white bulbs imbedded in plastic grapevines suspended from the ceiling and the backlit liquor rack behind the bar. The tables were draped with red and white checkered tablecloths and matching napkins. Soft, mandolin music was playing in the background and there was the faint scent of garlic and fresh baked bread. It was a place for good wine and intimate conversations. There were only a handful of patrons and as I looked around the room, a man stood and waved to us, motioning us over to his table. He was short and needed every square inch of his slightly crumpled blue suit. He was bald on the top and gray on the sides, with pale blue watery eyes. A pair of rimless glasses was perched about mid-way down his long beak of a nose and he peered over them like a librarian. He shook our hands warmly.

"Thank you so much for coming. Very nice to meet you, Mr. Macmillan."

He spoke with a British accent.

"You can call me Mark."

He turned to Megan.

"I'm sorry Miss. I don't know your name."

"I'm Megan. Wow you have a really..., I mean this is a really nice place."

She gave me a sideways glance. I was trying to keep a straight face.

"Hello Megan. I'm Hamilton. My friends call me Ham. It is not a reference, thankfully, to my acting skills, of which I assure you, I have none. Please sit down."

The waitress came over with a basket of bread and a plate of olive oil. Ham ordered a bottle of Sangiovese, and then made some recommendations from the menu. While Megan and I studied the entrees, he explained that this was his favorite restaurant in all of Charleston and then proceeded to give us a short history of the place. The waitress returned with the bottle and three glasses. She uncorked it and poured a small amount into Ham's glass. He put the glass up to his substantial nose and then took a sip. He nodded his head. After she had poured the three glasses, Ham held his aloft.

"Here's to the beginning of a rewarding endeavor!"

He took a long drink followed by a deep breath, allowing the air to escape slowly through his slightly parted lips. He looked at us both in turn as if trying to decide which was the driver and which the passenger on this strange journey we were about to embark on. He apparently decided to start with me.

"I have a rather long and, I think, very interesting story to tell you both. I am not going to ask you a lot of questions at this point, but I would at least like to confirm that you are in search of the same object that I am currently pursuing. May I confirm that you are looking for a book? A book of poetry?"

We looked at each other. Megan spoke.

"We're looking for a book. I thought you had it until I talked to Rachel. I don't really know much about it."

Ham nodded.

"Well no. I do not currently have the book and obviously you do not either, or we would not be having this conversation."

"We'd rather not comment on that." I said, a little wary of revealing too much before I knew what was going on. "I don't mean to be rude but may I ask you what your involvement is in this thing, Mr. Biers?"

"Please, call me Ham. That is a rather complicated discussion. If you don't mind, I would prefer to answer that question after you have heard what I have to say. Are we agreed?"

"Okay for now."

"Splendid. To begin, let me ask have you have ever heard of the Ruba'iyat of Omar Khayyam?"

Megan shook her head no.

"Sure it's a book of Islamic poetry."

"Well, that is how it is regarded by many today. Although not correctly. Omar Khayyam was actually a twelfth century Persian mathematician, astronomer, and poet. He was what is known as a Sufi or Dervish. It is a discipline that has its roots in Hinduism and predates Islam by many years. The aim is the reparation of the heart, and the turning away from the pursuit of material things so as to better know God. They practice with a kind of chanting called the dhika which is an endless repletion of the name of God. It is somewhat ironic that the book is now known as an Islamic text, if I may recite a quatrain for you."

A book of verses underneath the bough

A flask of wine, a loaf of bread and thou

Beside me singing in the wilderness

And wilderness is paradise enow

"Not exactly the Islamic ideal one would say. But nonetheless, what is important here is that a copy of the original Persian manuscript made its way to London in 1856 by means of one Edward Cowell, a noted scholar at the Bodleian Library, Oxford. He in turn convinced a well known translator of ancient texts to render the work in English. That man was Edward

Marlborough Fitzgerald. What is astounding about this part of the story is that Fitzgerald at this point had no facility with the Persian language whatsoever. More astounding than that, was that this man devoted the next twenty five years of his life learning the language and translating the verses into English. It would be difficult imagining such a thing happening today. I tell you all this by way of explaining the significance of the thing we are looking for."

"To continue, once the translation was finished, Fitzgerald offered the manuscript to Fraser's magazine, a literary publication of the day and to his great dismay was rejected. After several additional attempts to interest a publisher he eventually paid to have the manuscript published himself, and this was done by a small publisher and book shop owner named Bernard Quaritch. Once published, it unfortunately languished on a dusty shelf for many months until finally being relegated to what they called the penny bin. This was the equivalent of the discount rack in today's book stores. Imagine the crushing disappointment after devoting all that time. It's quite unimaginable really."

The waitress returned to the table with a large salad bowl and the conversation stopped while we served ourselves.

"In any case, this is where the story may have reasonably come to an end, except for the fortuitous arrival of one Dante Rosetti at Quaritche's book shop, who, upon digging around the penny bin came across the small book and was immediately transfixed. Now, Dante Rosetti was a well known writer, painter, and poet of the day and was the founder of the Pre-Raphaelite Brotherhood, a noted gathering of the brighter artists and literary lights of London. Through him the book made its way into the hands of such literary luminaries as Charles Swinburne, George Meredith, and John Ruskin. In short, the Ruba'iyat became one of the most widely read works of poetry of the age. It has been published frequently throughout the nineteenth and twentieth century until even today. All that by way of background."

He paused for a few moments and ate some of his salad, finishing with a long sip of his wine. He blotted at his mouth with his napkin and then placed it back on his lap.

"Now here is where the story begins to get interesting. You see it was quite fashionable in the late nineteenth and early twentieth century for a young swain to present a book of poetry to a lady to impress her with his sensitivity, not to mention his undying love and devotion, etcetera, etcetera, ad nauseam. The more elaborate and expensive the binding, of course, the greater the ardor of the suitor."

Megan smiled. "There's that word again. Suitor. It cracks me up."

Ham looked at her in silence for a moment, not quite understanding the comment. He smiled and continued.

"In any case, to profit from this tradition, many of the bookbinders in London set about trying to outdo each other in elaborate editions of some of the better known verses of the day. The Ruba'iyat found its way into the hands of one Francis Sangorski of the firm Sangorski and Sutcliffe, one of the most prominent bookbinders of the time. Mr. Sangorski believed he could make a small fortune by producing the most elegant and expensive book of verses ever beheld by the eyes of man and he set out to accomplish just that. After all, what could be more exotic and irresistible than a book of obscure Persian poetry? Well, the work took two years to complete and the results were astounding by any measure.

The cover consisted of a solid gold heart and a trio of gold winged peacocks encrusted by more than a thousand precious and semi-precious gems. There were rubies, garnets, turquoise, and topaz among others. Each of them individually set in a gold mounting. In addition there were inlays of silver, ivory and mahogany as well as hundreds of leather details in a variety of different grains and colors. The illustrations were done by Elihu Vedder, an expatriate American living in Rome. He was one of the most accomplished illustrators of the day. In short, it was a most remarkable piece of work and Mr. Sangorski expected to make a very pretty penny indeed. As luck would have it, and by the way as you will see, turns of bad luck seem to be woven into this saga like a sad tapestry, England became mired in a coal miners strike shortly before the work was finished. Since coal was the only fuel available to Londoners in this age, the result was to nearly cripple the British economy. Everything lost value and there was wide-spread unemployment and many business failures."

He paused and had some more of his wine.

"Now, Mr. Sangorski, after assessing the wretched state of England's economy, apparently decided he would have a better chance of hitting his mark in the United States and he put the work on a ship bound for New York. Upon arriving at customs in New York, and after a close examination of the book by some very circumspect customs agents, a duty was set on the work that was far beyond what Mr. Sangorski was prepared to pay. The book was promptly returned by ship to London and after a few insultingly low offers, in time was put up for public auction at Southebys. He expected a minimum of one thousand pounds. Not an insubstantial sum in those times. Instead, he was forced to settle for four hundred and fifty pounds to a New York book dealer named Gabriel Wells. Mr. Sangorski was so devastated by the results that he went into a deep depression and just a short time after the book was sold, he died while attempting to save a woman who was drowning. Some swore his death was actually a result of the final and most ironic indignity of this part of the tale. You see, Mr. Wells promptly had his new acquisition put aboard another ship bound for New York. That vessel was Her Majesty's Mail Ship Titanic."

I looked at Megan and then back at Ham. I started to say something but Ham interrupted me.

"I know, I know. You're thinking why in the hell did I just waste my time listening to this old fool go on about what is no doubt now just a pile of scraps and small jewels at the bottom of the Atlantic ocean. Well, just bear with me a moment and I will endeavor to enlighten you."

The waitress brought out the entrees and we began eating. Ham didn't speak for some time and Megan was nearly beside herself wanting to hear the rest of the story. We had almost finished before he began again.

"So where was I? Oh yes, the bottom of the Atlantic Ocean. At this point I need to tell you a little about the start of Titanic's voyage. Some of this is conjecture but the important facts are believed to be correct as you will see as the story continues. Titanic being a new ship also had a new crew. Some had sailed with captain Smith before and many with the White Star Line but the nature of the work requires hands to move from ship to ship as opportunities arise. The result was that, for the most part, these men did not know each other. Officers did not know the men under their command and vise-versa. It was therefore quite easy for a member of the crew to board the ship and remain unnoticed for some time. Many people think the Titanic left Southampton, England and sailed directly for

New York. This is not the case. The Titanic sailed at noon on April 10th 1912 bound for Cherbourg in France, where she arrived around suppertime. Here she boarded quite a few new passengers and mail bound for America."

"She didn't depart again until 9 PM. She then made for the Irish port of Queenstown. The place is now known as Cobh, as the Irish are not entirely fond of the Queen in recent times. In any case the Titanic dropped anchor in Queenstown harbor at 1PM on the 11th. Here she was boarded by a large number of young Irish men and women bound for the new world and an additional batch of mail. In addition, while the passengers were being boarded, the captain allowed a number of Irish lace merchants to board where they were permitted to sell their wares. It is known that Jacob Astor, one of the wealthiest men in the world at that time, purchased a lace jacket for the tidy sum of eight hundred dollars. In short, survivors reported a scene of great chaos as the passengers and crew and the merchants all milled about. Also, below decks the crew was still frantically trying to clean up construction debris left behind by the Belfast men who had built her. When the ship was finally ready to get underway, the lace sellers departed on the tender. Hidden among them were an able seaman and fireman named J. Coffy who was a denizen of Queenstown and apparently came down with a severe case of home sickness and decided not to undertake the voyage. Lucky for him. With him was another member of the crew listed as Eric Wood. This was later found to be a fictitious name."

"Now here is what is believed to have happened. The cargo of the Titanic was an odd assortment of all sorts of things. There were 5 Grand Pianos, 30 cases of golf clubs and tennis racquets, a cask of fine China bound for Tiffany's, a Renault automobile belonging to first class passenger Walter Porter, seventy-two cases of Dragon's Blood, which no one has been able to satisfactorily explain to me, and ... AND, four cases of opium. Now opium was a completely legal commodity in those days. It was used extensively in medicine but there was also a lucrative underground trade in the stuff. So the story goes that an Irish stoker, by the name of Sean McMichael, conspired with some compatriots to remove a fair amount of the stuff for the purposes of private enterprise. He boarded the ship in Southampton, shortly before lading was complete and hid himself in the cargo hold. Once under way, he riffled through the cargo until he found the opium. He loaded as much of the stuff as he could manage into a seaman's duffle bag and then waited. It is said that he slept that night in the back seat of the Renault. The next day when the ship arrived at Queenstown, he simply took his kit and walked off the ship. But opium wasn't all he had put in the duffle bag. You see our lad was apparently of the mind that for taking all the risk, he was entitled to a little something extra. During his search of the cargo, we believe he happened to come across a beautiful little book of poetry that fit nicely into his bag. He had no idea of its value, but he was sure it was worth a lot."

"That sounds a little speculative to me. How could you know any of this is true?"

"Well, I am not 100% sure of any of these details, Mark, but there is evidence to support what I have just told you. If you don't mind, I'll get to that shortly."

I nodded.

"In any case, our lad and his cronies were no doubt in a terrible sweat for what would happen when the ship arrived in New York. There would be an investigation and who knows what they would uncover. They were no doubt among the very few people in the world who were happy with the news that the Titanic had perished at sea. They had just pulled off the perfect crime and not a worry in the world. Now,

142

one would imagine the opium was easy enough to get rid of and at a 100% profit, thank you very much. But the book was a different story. No Irish seaman was going to march himself into a rare bookstore with something like that. What he did instead was to hide the book in a hollowed out section of one of those old Bibles that almost nobody read anyway since they were almost too damned big and heavy to take off the shelf. One supposes he decided it would be better to let the dust settle for a while, at least until he figured out how to sell the thing. Unfortunately for out lad, this is where the story takes a tragic turn. It is also the origin of rumors that the book is cursed."

"There's a curse?" Megan asked

"Well, that issue is up for debate. You will have to draw your own conclusion. You see, a few months after the Titanic was lost an Irish writer by the name of Patrick Gaffney found himself imprisoned in Dublin for non-payment of his debts. In these times you could be held indefinitely, even die in debtor's prison until you paid up. There were no personal bankruptcy laws in Ireland at the time and no sympathy for debtors. In any case, during his incarceration he met a young merchant seaman by the name of Sean McMichael who had been convicted of murder and was awaiting execution. Over a span of several weeks they became friends and Mr. McMichael eventually told him how he had ended up in such dire straits. Mr. Gaffney, in time, was able to settle his debt and was released, but not before witnessing the execution. He turned Sean McMichael's tale into a short story which manuscript can apparently still be found in the Library at Trinity College in Dublin. The story is quite fascinating in its own right and it supports most of the details of the tale I have just told you. Would you like to hear it or should I just move on to the matter at hand?"

"I'd like to hear it." Megan said.

"Very well. The story goes that our lad Sean had fallen in love with a beautiful young Irish lass named Kathleen Fylan. These were difficult times in Ireland and young people were leaving in droves to find opportunity in the new world. They knew that there was no future for them in Ireland and they endeavored to scratch together enough money to emigrate to America. Sean was eventually able to find work on a black gang, feeding the coal fired boilers on the newly constructed Titanic. A few weeks prior to the Titanic's departure he left Dublin bound for the Southampton docks, with a promise to Kathleen that after the round trip voyage to America, he would return for her with enough money for them to depart together for a new life. However, while waiting for the ship to sail, Sean met up with some lads who were involved in the illegal opium trade and were looking for a way to remove some quantity of the stuff they knew had been laded onto Titanic. Now by all accounts, Sean was an honest lad but he knew that Kathleen's very existence was in peril. The Fylan's were poor farmers living hand to mouth as tenants on lands owned by a British lord. They were known as 'tenants at will' since they could be thrown off the land at any time, sometimes in the middle of the night with their one-room cabin burnt to the ground. Apparently this was soon to be the fate of the Fylan clan. After seeing Titanic's sailing schedule, Sean thought he had found a way to get the money he needed to afford passage for he and Kathleen without having to sail all the way to New York and back first. Subsequently, he and his newfound cronies hatched the plan I have already described to you."

"Now it turns out that the man who owned the Fylan's tenant farm was named Ian Chadwick and being of advancing years had recently turned over the management of his lands to his son Arthur who was in his early twenties at the time. Arthur traveled to Ireland to see the property for himself, whereupon he beheld the lovely Kathleen for the first time and decided he wanted her for himself. Now Kathleen resisted Arthur's advances steadfastly until in apparent desperation, he told her that if she didn't surrender to him he would burn down her cabin and throw her family out into the road. Not a very noble act, but then there never was much nobility among the Nobles of the time. Of any time some would say. In any case, Kathleen was a virtuous young lass but she was no fool and she knew the very survival of her family was at stake. She was smart and courageous enough to make the best of a very dire situation. She told Arthur that she would not marry him, but she would submit to his desires one time and one time only if in return he would give her father and her family the legal right to farm the land they occupied without fear of eviction as long as the family survived. In addition, she demanded enough money to book passage to New York and an additional sum for her and Sean to start a new life. It was a steep price, but apparently one that Arthur could not refuse."

"What an asshole."

"Indeed. However, Arthur did at least uphold his end of the bargain as did Kathleen. Once the deed was done, not wanting to face her father after committing a sin that would bring disgrace to her family, she immediately made her way to Queenstown harbor. There, the courageous girl booked passage on the Titanic and waited for the ship and her lover to arrive. So it was that Kathleen boarded the Titanic, just as her lover Sean was making his escape. Sean told Mr. Gaffney that as he boarded the tender to depart Titanic, he looked up at the throng of passengers at the rail and got a brief glimpse of what he thought was a most lovely and familiar face in the crowd. Never suspecting that it was Kathleen and that it would be the last time he would ever see her in this world."

"Now you can imagine his horror and despair when he learned of the loss of the great ship and found out how Kathleen had come to be aboard. He immediately sought out and confronted Arthur Chadwick. There was an altercation and Arthur was knocked to the ground and struck his head on a rock. He never regained consciousness. Needless to say, there would be no mercy for a common Irish lad who had just killed the son of an English lord. Sean was condemned to hang for the murder. He confided in Mr. Gaffney that he was happy to pass over to the other side if it meant he could finally reunite with his lost love. He was also convinced that it was the theft of the book that had turned his life upside down and caused

147

Kathleen to take his place on the ill-fated voyage. Mr. Gaffney writes that as Sean stood on the gallows he was asked if he had any last words. Sean stated his remorse at the death of Arthur Chadwick and asked for God's forgiveness. But then he went into a tirade about a book that had been the cause of all of his grief. Before plunging to his death he rambled on about some old bible and the evil thing that was inside of it. The crowd thought he was cursing the scripture itself and Sean went to his death to the sound of the crowd's very vocal displeasure at his blasphemy."

"Wow that's incredible." Megan said. "Is that true?"

"As I said, we cannot be certain of any of these details, however the story does fit with the other known facts about the book and is from an independent source."

"I wonder how many stories there are like that. Things and people we'll never know about."

"Many, no doubt, on the Titanic alone. I'm sure at least a few people missed the sailing through odd circumstances and perhaps others were allowed passage as a result. One of those who missed the sailing was the Industrialist J.P. Morgan, the actual owner of the ship. As you said, we will never know. In any case, that is the origin of the supposed curse on the great book. The history of the book since that time has done nothing to dispel the claim, but I'll let you make up your own minds about that. What we do know for certain is this. The Bible containing the stolen book, at some point, ended up in a pile of abandoned goods and other old books in a warehouse in Dublin. Apparently in all the intervening years, no one ever bothered to open the clasps of the massive bible to look inside. In these times, large old family bibles were a dime a dozen. Even today they are not of much value because there were so many printed. Anyway, twenty seven years later, the bible along with some number of additional old books, was purchased in a lot by an another enterprising New York book trader. The books were promptly crated up and shipped back to the states. The name of that book trader was Abraham Weiss. Husband of one Sarah Weiss and father of Annabel Weiss of New York city."

9

Megan gasped. "You mean that is what we're looking for?"

"That is my belief, yes. It is generally referred to today as 'The Great Omar' and is one of the most famous bindings ever produced. And as I have explained, some say the most cursed."

"How much is it worth?"

"That my dear, is a complicated question. First, it would have to be determined whether we are talking about the first edition. You see, the design of the original binding was lost for many years. Eventually it was rediscovered by a man named Stanley Bray. He was the nephew of George Sutcliffe, Sangorski's partner, and he apprenticed under him at the bindery. Mr. Bray produced a copy of the original binding, apparently exact in every detail. The second version was completed just prior to the start of World War II. In another tragic twist of fate, this second version was placed in a safe in a bank vault for protection and that vault and safe were destroyed by a German bomb during the Blitz. The book was never found and was assumed destroyed. We also know that a third copy was completed by the same Stanley Bray and that copy can now be seen in the British Library. So we are left with two choices. Either the story I have told you is essentially true and the book we are following is the one taken from the Titanic, or the story of the second copy being lost during the Blitz was a fabrication and what we have, or hope to have, is the duplicate."

"So who actually owns it?"

"That is the most complicated question of all. Let us assume we are talking about the original Great Omar and the story is true. The first question would be whether or not it was insured by the White Star Line. No such book is noted on the cargo manifest nor is there a known bill of lading for it. So even if there were a policy, the book would not be covered by it."

"Wouldn't that mean it couldn't have been in the cargo hold?"

"Not necessarily. Some of the passengers boarded with quite a lot of baggage, literally and figuratively one supposes. One first class passenger who boarded in Cherbourg is known to have had sixteen steamer trunks with him. Those would no doubt have been placed in the hold and would not necessarily show up on a cargo manifest. Which brings us back to the question of private insurance. I have not been able to determine whether Mr. Wells had the work insured prior to shipment. The current belief is that he did not. If, however there were a claim paid, then the book would now be the property of the insurance company. The historical record shows that the entire cargo was valued at something just over $420,000. Keep in mind Mr. Wells only paid 450 British Pounds for the book. Not an enormous sum and quite probably not insured. After all, the Titanic was 'unsinkable' as we all know."

Ham paused and took another sip of his wine.

"The next question would be proof of ownership. There do not seem to be any records that show a discernible difference between the first and second renderings. Mr. Sangorski and Mr. Sutcliffe are long gone as is Mr. Bray. Mr. Wells is also deceased, so it would be up to his heirs, assuming there are any, to prove that the book that has suddenly emerged out of the shadows is the first edition that was sold at auction. Even if that is determined, it would have to be proven that the book had been stolen as we propose, or whether it may have been miraculously preserved and salvaged during one of the recent visits to the sunken vessel. In that case salvage rules would apply. It is known that some 300 artifacts have been recovered from the wreck to date. Some quite valuable. Even though this is an extremely remote possibility, it could sufficiently muddy the waters to make a claim of ownership difficult. After all to some, a salvage scenario may be no more unlikely than the story of some Irish stoker pinching the thing out of the cargo hold."

"The greatest difficulty, I believe, would be proving that it was not the second edition, and therefore owned by the heirs of Mr. Bray or generally by the heirs of the binding business if there are any. If all else fails, then possession is, as they say, nine-tenths of the law. In that case, the rightful owner would be the last known purchaser of the work. That would be Abraham Weiss, or more precisely, the heirs of Abraham Weiss. Now I know that you were provided with my name by Ms. Annabel Weiss through her friend Rachel. Rachel advised me of expect your visit. So, I think now would be an opportune time to ask you what exactly would be you're involvement in this affair?"

"She gave it to me."

"Annabel Weiss gave you the Great Omar? That is an extraordinary claim, my dear. Do you have any proof of that?"

"Yeah. I have a letter from her. Anyway, you can ask her yourself."

"Unfortunately, that is no longer possible."

"Why not?"

"I'm afraid Ms. Weiss has passed away."

Megan started to cry. "Annabel died? How, when did it happen?"

It happened yesterday at some time. I received a call from Rachel this afternoon. She asked me, by the way, to pass along her condolences and to ask you to be very careful of anyone expressing interest in the book."

"How did it happen?"

"Apparently she died of a heart attack. However it was most probably a result of the invasion and ransacking of her apartment in New York City. It is my belief that whoever did this is pursuing the same book we are. I'm very sorry to have to give you this news."

"Oh my, God. She knew it was going to happen. She was really shook up the last time I saw her. She said she didn't have much time left. I can't believe it."

"If it's any comfort, I am told it was a massive coronary and she likely went very quickly. There were no signs of trauma on her body."

Megan sat back and cried softly. I put my arm around her. After a few minutes she wiped the tears from her eyes and looked over at Ham.

"Did you know Annabel?"

"No, I never had the pleasure. But I have corresponded with her on several occasions in the past few weeks with regard to this matter. She seemed like a very dear woman and I am deeply saddened as you are. I would have postponed our discussion to a later time when I received news of her passing, but I had no idea when you would be arriving and no way to contact you. She did not, however, make any mention of giving the book to anyone. I would be interested in seeing the letter you have mentioned?"

Megan started to respond, but I stopped her.

"It's in a safe place. We'll be prepared to show it to you when it's appropriate."

"Are you related to Ms. Weiss in any way, Megan?"

"No, we're friends that's all."

"Very well. That shouldn't create any real difficulties for now at least. It may, however, become a matter of some importance if we find the Great Omar. I suggest you keep this letter in a secure place and tell no one about it. Hopefully, Ms. Weiss also has made mention of this in her will or at least by letter to her attorney, should it be needed."

"I don't mean to sound rude, but how do we know we can trust you?"

"That's a fair question, Mark. But I suppose you will have to take that on faith. I will tell you that it was I who located Ms. Weiss and informed her that it was possible the great book had once again come to light. My proposal to her was that I would search for the book and, if found, would arrange to sell it to the highest bidder at my standard commission. I would not have contacted Ms. Weiss had I some intent to cheat her out of something that belongs to her. I could easily sell the book as my own possession without her being any the wiser. I chose to take the honorable path here."

"So how much is it worth?"

"The unofficial answer to that question is that it is priceless, which means, were it to go up for auction, some initial and very substantial opening bid would be established and then collectors would have at it. My best guess, if it sold at auction, could be upwards of ten million dollars."

Megan sat back in her chair. She looked as though she were about to faint.

"But wouldn't proof of ownership have to be established before it could go up for auction?" I asked.

"That is what is known as an articles provenance. A string of ownership with verification that goes back through the history of the item.   In this case with such a sketchy background, my guess is that legal fight could go on until we ourselves are all dead and buried. Which is why it will never go to auction."

"So how is it worth anything then?"

"It will be sold to a private buyer. I already have a substantial offer in hand for the book, assuming I can produce it. An open question at this point."

"Isn't that illegal?" Megan asked.

"That is also an important question. In this instance, as I said, possession is nine-tenths of the law and in any case this is a problem for the buyer, and the seller. Not for me."

Megan looked a little indignant. "Couldn't you be arrested for selling stolen goods?"

"Well, I am not actually selling anything. The seller in this case would be the estate of Ms. Weiss. I am merely an agent. Ms. Weiss kept documents to show that she came into possession of the book quite legally. If the story I have just told you is accurate, the only person who stole the Great Omar prior to Ms. Weiss coming into possession of it was Sean McMichael and he apparently was amply punished for his transgression. Disagreements regarding an objects provenance do not amount to theft."

"So is this what you do?" I asked. "Sell stolen art."

Ham gave me a long look over his glasses and cleared his throat before he replied.

"Let me describe the landscape of my world to you. There is a thriving commerce in rare and expensive objects of art in this world. Always has been and probably always will be. Wealthy men and women seem to need to surround themselves with these kinds of objects. In some way I think they see them as a kind of mirror that reflects their value back upon themselves. Reassurance, I suppose, of ones worth. Of course, many of these people purchase art as an investment, hoping it will appreciate over time, as it often does. There are others who simply love great art and are blessed with the means to acquire it. Fortunately, wealth is not required to appreciate great art. Only to possess it. My work brings me into contact with many people of means. Wealthy people are a strange and different breed. I have always been rather amused at the fact that many of these individuals would just as soon spit on an actual artist as give him the time of day, and yet they are prepared to pay enormous amounts of money for what they produce. It is one of the great conundrums of our modern world. A society that fails to respect its artists is on a path to mediocrity, I believe. Great civilizations are remembered by the art they produced."

"I am not a collector of great art, with the exception of a few modest pieces that have particular significance to me. I am simply a broker. There are many unscrupulous players in this game that I play and some are very dangerous. Some men in my position actually commission the theft of art objects from museums and private collectors on contract. Many more have no hesitancy to sell known, stolen objects of art if they can make a profit. Some will not stop at murder and worse to get what they want. I am not one of those men. I have never, knowingly, sold a stolen art object to anyone. I am not greedy. I make a very good living dealing in private sales of objects whose provenance is known or at least which cannot be shown to be illegally obtained. Most often these items are sold privately because the buyers do not wish to be publicly identified, sometimes for tax reasons, which is also not my concern. I am scrupulous about paying the taxes on my income and that, along with the completion of the necessary paperwork, is the limit of my responsibility, providing what I am selling is not stolen. You may question whether selling 'The Great Omar' is ethical, but I ask you, who really is entitled to profit from this object. The heirs of some long dead businessman who know nothing about it, have never set eyes on it and who have done nothing to earn the right to own it, or someone who purchased it legally, albeit accidentally, even though he may not have appreciated its value at the time."

Megan spoke again. "Yeah, but if some private collector has it hidden away, the rest of the people in the world never get the chance to see it."

"That's true Megan, but not unusual. A tremendous amount of great art in the world is not held in museums. It is owned by governments and wealthy individuals, out of the public view. Also, in this particular case this is really not a valid objection. A copy of 'The Great Omar' sits in the British Library. Anyone is free to go look at it. They don't even charge admission. I have seen it many times and it is indeed beautiful. I seriously doubt that there is anyone currently living in this world capable of distinguishing this copy from the original."

The waitress came back and asked if we wanted coffee, but we declined. Ham asked for the check. We sat in silence for a moment. Each to our own thoughts. I looked over at Ham.

"So what are you proposing, Mr. Biers?"

"Please, call me Ham."

"Okay Ham. What do you want?"

"Well, that depends on many things, most of which are unknown at present. At this point however, if you both agree, I would suggest we conclude our discussion for tonight and continue tomorrow at some time. There is much more to this story and it's been a very long day for me. I think I've given you quite a lot to think about as it is. I can see, also, that the news about Ms. Weiss' passing has affected you deeply Megan and it would be good if you had some time to come to grips with it. I would like to suggest that we meet again tomorrow, let's say around noon. If not, whenever you are ready. I would like you to take some time to consider what I've told you so far, before I finish telling you about the book."

I looked over at Megan and she nodded her head.

"You will have a decision to make at some point and it is not as simple as it may seem. The Great Omar is an object of great value but one with a very troubled history. The lives of many who have come into contact with the book have been lost. I do not believe in cursed objects per se, but in my line of work I have come across a few items that are undeniably associated with financial ruin and untimely death. Perhaps it is no more than coincidence. I don't pretend to know. They say an artist always imbues his creation with something of himself. There certainly is some power in a great work of art. The power to invoke thought and emotion in those who behold it. And among some, the overwhelming desire to possess it. Perhaps there is something about the Great Omar that brings out the worst in people. Perhaps there is some actual power in the despair of star-crossed lovers and the curse of a condemned man about to hang. Or perhaps the book was destined to come to rest at the bottom of the sea after all, and its true owners are the one thousand five hundred and thirteen souls who perished on board the Titanic, including Kathleen Fylan, if that was her real name. Maybe they are aggrieved of its loss and awaiting its return. These things you will need to balance against the wealth The Great Omar would bring you. It would certainly change your financial fortunes in a single turn. This may all seem preposterous to you and probably does, but I have seen many strange things in my career. I have knowledge of certain events which I cannot explain. Which no one can explain."

10

We returned to the hotel room sometime after ten. Megan was silent on the walk back through the old town. She went immediately out onto the balcony and leaned against the balustrade. The lights of the town were illuminating the beautiful, antebellum houses with a soft, almost golden glow and a warm breeze stirred the air with the scent of the harbor and the taste of the sea. It was a beautiful evening, but there is a melancholy feel to Old Charleston at night. The stately buildings seem full of secrets and sleep, and simmering regret. I wanted to ask Megan how she felt about our meeting with Ham but I sensed she needed some time to herself and I didn't approach her. I decided to clean up instead. I took my kit into the bathroom and washed my face. I sprayed some shaving cream on my fingers but then stopped for a moment and looked at my reflection in the mirror. For an instant I didn't recognize the man looking back at me. It was as if I had entered another existence. One that had swallowed me so completely that I couldn't remember what my life had felt like just a few days earlier. I lingered in the shower for a good while, letting the warm water soak away some of the stress. When I emerged I put on one of the bathrobes and stepped out onto the balcony. Megan had gone again to that far away place she retreated to when she didn't want to look at the world. She didn't seem to know I was standing there with her.

"Are you all right, Megan?" I asked at last.

She turned and looked at me, her eyes red and swollen.

"Yeah. I'll be okay. I'm just amazed at how much the news about Annabel shook me up. I didn't know her very long at all, but it felt like my mother died all over again."

She started to cry, and I put my arm around her shoulders. She rested her head on my chest and we stood there quietly for a long while. Finally she looked up at me.

"Thank you for being here with me. I'm just lost. I don't know what to do, and I'm afraid. I haven't felt like this in a long, long time."

I kissed her on the top of the head.

"You're not alone Megan. Let's go back inside. It's getting a little chilly out here."

I sat down on one of the double beds and she sat beside me, staring down at her feet. After a while she looked up at me, studying my face as she always did. Searching perhaps for some reassurance. I had none to offer.

"So what do you think of him?" She asked.

"Ham? I guess I'm not really sure yet. For the most part I guess I believe him but who knows. He could be running some kind of scam."

"I thought that too for a while, but it's true he didn't have to tell anyone about the book. He did contact Annabel."

"Yes, but it's probably to his advantage to have someone with a valid claim to the book. I don't know?"

"I'm not sure I want it."

"No? Do you believe it's cursed?"

"I don't know what I believe. Maybe because of the way Annabel died. I can't imagine how terrified she must have been when they

166

broke into her apartment. They frightened her to death. That used to be just something people said. I don't know what to do."

"That was horrible, but there's really nothing you could have done for her. Nothing you can do now."

"I could talk to the police. Maybe I could help them find the bastards who did that to her."

"You could talk to them but you really don't have much information to give. Just that you knew she was afraid."

"I could tell them about that guy who was following me."

"You could, but you don't know if he had anything to do with the break-in. You said he didn't threaten you at all. We don't really even know if the break-in happened before or after Annabel died. I'm sure the police know, but we really know nothing of use to them."

"I guess you're right. I just feel like we should do something."

"There is one thing we should do as soon as we can. We should call Rachel and see if she has the name and number of Annabel's lawyer. It would be good to know there is someone who could authenticate the letter she gave you and to see if Annabel told him about giving you the book. He might have more information about the police investigation also."

"What should we do with the letter for now, to keep it safe?"

"I think I'll make some copies tomorrow morning. We'll give a copy to Ham tomorrow and I'll mail one to my lawyer back in Vermont just in case. We'll open up a safe deposit box in your name and keep the original there until you need it."

"Here in Charleston?"

"Well, that depends on what you want to do now. It sounds like it's going to take a little time to find the book. If you want, you could come down to Boca Raton with me until we get it all sorted out. It's up to you. There's plenty of room at the condo. You could open a safe deposit box down there."

"I don't want to be a nuisance. I just don't know where else to go."

"Not at all. I'd enjoy the company."

"Okay. If you really don't mind. Anyway, I want to split it with you. The money I mean."

"No, I can't let you do that. This is your inheritance, Megan. I couldn't take your money."

"I don't care. I wouldn't be able to do this without you. You deserve half of it. No matter how much there is. Who knows what kind of crap we're going to have to go through to get this book. You can't just do this for nothing. I don't know why you would want to help me anyway. I mean there you were driving down to Florida for a vacation, free as a bird and you pick up this crazy homeless chick and now you're in the middle of some big stupid drama. I wouldn't be surprised if you just got into your car and took off. Why are you helping me anyway? Why would you put yourself through all this crap for somebody you don't even know? Is it because Rachel put some kind of guilt trip on you? I don't get it."

"Do I have to give you a reason? Because I'm not sure I have one. Not one I can put into words, anyway. Rachel said we were both going through changes in our lives and we needed to help each other. She was right about the changes. I think she was right about needing each other too."

"What do you need me for?"

"I think I need somebody to care about, Megan. Somebody to help me get out of my own head. I'm amazed at how much has changed since I met you. How much more alive I feel. Besides, I like you Megan. I like who you are. Your honesty and you courage and the way you look at the world."

"You're afraid of the curse aren't you?"

"No. I don't believe in curses either."

"But all of those people who died because of this book and now Annabel too. How could that be a coincidence?"

"Who knows? I think these things tend to take on a life of their own. If a few bad things happen in a place or around some object, people start to make connections. Most of the time it's all the work of some overactive imaginations. Still, I think we need to be careful."

Megan stood up suddenly.

"I'm going to have a shower, do you mind?"

"No, I'll set the alarm in case I fall asleep before you're done. I think you'll feel better about all of this in the morning."

I had already turned out the lights. The soft glow from the old town cast dim shadows on the walls and the curtains moved in the gentle breeze. The streets were quiet except for the whisper of an occasional car passing by on the cobbled street below. The vestige of someone's solitary journey through the night. My head was still spinning with the events that had taken hold of my life since I met Megan. It didn't seem possible. It didn't seem like there was even enough time for it all to have happened. Just a chance meeting at a rest stop on the turnpike and suddenly I was knee deep in something I couldn't even fully understand. More than that, I had no idea what I was doing. I had developed strong feelings for Megan which surprised me a little, but I couldn't figure out what I should do about it. I didn't think we could ever have any kind of serious relationship. She was too young for me to begin with and then there was the difference in the way we saw the world. She hadn't given me any indication she was interested in me in that way either and I didn't expect her to. But she was nothing like the women I had met since I became single again. There were no games about her. No hidden agenda. I thought she was probably the most honest person I had ever known. I wanted her to fit into my life in some way. I just couldn't imagine how. And then there was the drama with Walt that I couldn't get my head around. He had always been a bit of a risk taker. More than me for sure, but he had never been reckless. Taking off like he had. Leaving Jen and the kids behind. It just made no sense to me. There was something going on. Something that wasn't good. And then there was the evening I had just spent with Jennifer. I could never do that to Walt but I sensed Jen had started to drift away from him and I couldn't deny I still had strong feelings for her. I didn't know what to do with any of it.

I had just started to drift off when the bathroom door opened. Megan switched off the fan and the lights. The room returned to darkness. She seemed to glow in the moonlight as she passed by the open draperies. Like a spirit, coming to me in a dream. In a moment she was standing next to my bed in a cloud of warm vapor, looking down at me with a towel around her body and a question on her lips. She didn't wait for an answer. In a single moment, the towel was on the floor and she was next to me, her hand on my back. Her eyes locked onto mine in the dim light, honest and unwavering, and unimaginably sad. She buried her head against my shoulder and began to sob. I held on to her as the grief poured from her in waves and her hot tears ran across my chest. It seemed to me then, that an entire lifetime of loss and regret, of pain and fear had finally burst forth from her like a flood. I felt her try to hold it back but she didn't have the strength. All she could manage was to hold onto me as if she feared she would drown in her own sorrow. And as her soft, warm body melted into mine I began to lose the sense of where I ended and where she began. Until I felt like I was holding onto her soul.

11

Ham was sitting on a park bench by the Battery. He was dressed exactly as he had been the night before and he looked like he had slept in his clothes. It was a beautiful, clear day and Megan seemed to be in good spirits. I had awakened to find her back in her own bed. She didn't mention what had passed between us the night before and she suddenly seemed a little shy around me. As we were leaving the room she put her arms around me briefly and whispered 'thank you'. No more was said about it.

"How are you feeling today, Megan?" Ham asked.

"I'm much better, thanks."

We walked for a while, looking out at the harbor and making small talk. Ham knew the entire history of Charleston and he seemed to like to rattle off obscure facts and little known tales, including the blockade of the harbor by

Blackbeard in the early seventeen hundreds. Eventually we made our way to a small park and sat at one of the picnic tables.

"So, what are you thinking after our conversation last night?"

"It's an interesting story. I guess we'd like to hear the rest of it."

"Do you have any questions?"

"Not at the moment."

"Do you. Megan?"

"I just want you to look me in the eye and tell me this isn't some kind of scam we're getting ourselves into."

"I'm not here to cheat you or hurt you, Megan. It is not in my nature to live that way. I don't know how I can convince you of that. For me, aside from any profit I may make from the sale of the book, this is very much about the process. The thrill of the chase so to speak. Finding something of great value that has been lost in time. It's what makes my life interesting. I don't consider myself a wealthy man, although some may disagree. I do have quite enough to live a comfortable life for as long as I may reasonably expect to breathe the free air. I have no desire to over-burden myself with objects, no matter what their value. Also in this case, I admit I will get some degree of satisfaction from seeing the book go to someone who will benefit from it, rather than to someone who will keep it locked away in a safe somewhere. Even if that is what eventually happens to the Great Omar."

"I just wanted to hear you say it. It means something to me to hear it."

"I understand completely. So shall I continue? Is there anything else you want to know?"

Megan shook her head.

"I'll pick up where I left it last night then, if you don't mind. You see the Great Omar was not yet prepared to come into the light willingly, or without a good deal more chaos. As you may be aware, Abraham Weiss unfortunately never returned from his trip to Europe. After leaving Dublin he traveled to London and then Warsaw, presumably in search of more rare books. By 1939 European Jews were fleeing by the thousands and many were prepared to sell their family heirlooms for a tenth of their value to get the cash they needed. Mr. Weiss, being an American citizen, I'm sure assumed he had nothing to fear. Unfortunately for him and for many millions of others, he was unable to escape when Poland was invaded by the Nazis. The family received no further word from him. The crate of books he had purchased in Dublin, however, did finally make its way safely across the Atlantic. A minor miracle in itself considering the U-boat attacks. The crate was delivered to Mr. Weiss's book shop in the Williamsburg section of the city, and there it sat, unopened, awaiting his return. Of course, Sarah Weiss could not bring herself to believe her husband was lost. She kept the bookstore open until after the war ended. By then she had to finally accept the worst. In 1947 she decided to close the store. She evidently had the good sense to open the old bible and set eyes on the Great Omar for the first time in some thirty five years. What a moment that must have been. Unfortunately, she immediately took the book around to several rare book dealers to see what it was worth. Within a week her shop was broken into and the small safe containing the Great Omar was stolen. A policeman who happened upon the crooks removing the safe was shot and killed. Once again, the great book had disappeared into the shadows, again taking a life, and not the last one either."

"Now after the robbery in New York, nothing is heard about the book until December of 1948, in Australia of all places."

"How did it get there?" Megan asked.

"Well, actually it most likely didn't, as you will see. On the morning of December first 1948, a man was found dead on Somerton Beach near Adelaide Australia. There was no identification on the body and all the labels had been removed from his clothing. There was no sign of foul play and no toxins were discovered in the body. There was, however, massive bleeding in all the major organs and the coroner concluded it was likely a case of poisoning by some agent that was undetectable if not found very shortly after death. Possibly Digitalis. The man had been dead since the previous evening at least. It was believed that he had been poisoned at some other location because there were signs in the esophagus of extensive vomiting, but no indication of that on or near the body. Later, the police found his suitcase that had been checked at the Adelaide train station. They found that the identification tag was missing and the labels had also been removed from all the clothing. They did find a tie with the name T. Keane on it, and this lead was investigated thoroughly. Nothing turned up. A jacket found in the suitcase was sewn in a method called featherstitching which was done by machinery only used in the United States at that time. The police were pretty certain that the murder victim was either American or at least had come from America. It was a complete mystery and is considered an open case even today."

"In any event, upon further examination of the man's clothing, a small rolled up piece of paper was found in a hidden pocket sewn into his pants. It turned out that on the paper was printed the words Tamam Shud. This is translated as 'ended' or 'finished' in Persian and they are the last words of the Ruba'iyat of Omar Khayyam. When this fact was released to the public, a man came forward and told the police he had found a volume of the Ruba'iyat in the back seat of his unlocked car that had been parked overnight near where the body was found. He had no idea where it had come from. He showed the book to the police and the scrap of paper had indeed been torn from this book. Moreover, the book was a limited edition of the original Fitzgerald translation, but it was not the Great Omar. In addition, written lightly in pencil on the last page was some kind of code. The police did not know what to make of it. Over the years everyone from military intelligence to psychics to mathematicians has attempted to translate the code, but to no avail. In all these intervening years, the code was never broken and most experts agreed it was just a fragment of some larger message and too incomplete to decipher. There was a military base nearby and it was originally thought the dead man may have been a spy. Nothing of the sort was ever proven."

Ham removed a notepad and pen from his jacket pocket. He wrote a string of letters on an open page.

"You have this memorized?"

"I have been on the trail of this book for many years Mark, and have spent hours laboring over this fragment."

He passed it over to us.

"As you can see, it seems to be just a meaningless string of letters."

WRGOABABD

WTBIMPANETP

MLIABOAIAQC

ITTMTSAMSTGAB

"So, what? Did you figure it out?" Megan asked.

"First, let me show you something else my investigation has turned up. It is a photocopy of a Telegram and I would like you to read it. Please note the date of this transmission is Sept 4, 1948"

I took the telegram and looked at it for a few moments before I began reading.

WE REQUEST G.O. AUTHENTICATED BY AUTHORITY BEFORE DECISION. (STOP)

WILL TENDER BID IF MY PEOPLE AGREE NOTIFY EARLIEST TIME POSSIBLE. (STOP)

MUST LEARN IF AVAILABLE BEFORE OUR ARRIVAL IN AUGUST QUEBEC CANADA. (STOP)

INTEND TRAVEL TO MIAMI TO SEE ARTICLE MYSELF SHOULD T.G. ACCEPT BID. (STOP)

Ham continued. "This telegram was found among some belongings of another man, now also deceased. He was a known dealer in stolen antiquities that lived in the Miami area. My belief is that G.O. refers to the Great Omar. Do you notice anything interesting about the message?"

We both looked at it again.

"What?" Megan said, after a few seconds.

"Take my pen please and circle the first letter of each word in the Telegram."

Megan started to circle the letters and then stopped suddenly.

"Oh my god. It's the same letters as in the code."

I looked at the message again and then shook my head.

"That's a little far fetched, don't you think?"

"Well, at first I was pretty skeptical myself, but there is no denying the letters do indeed exactly match the words in the telegram. I am not a statistician, but my guess is the odds of something like that occurring at random are extremely small. This is a most basic example of what is known among cryptologists as an idiot code. Most code breakers would assume that this was some sort of substitution cipher, where each letter represents a different letter in a sentence. An idiot code is one in which the letters don't necessarily stand for anything. They have meaning only to two people. The sender and the receiver. There is no real way to decipher it, since it is only used once."

"Okay, but what good is it to know the first letter of each word?"

"My guess is that it was a simple way for the potential buyer in Australia to verify that the person he was meeting was actually the representative of the seller in the United States. He would have been aware that the object he was seeking had been stolen and a policeman killed. He would have wanted to exhibit extreme caution in dealing with people he did not know. Otherwise, a police detective, for example, might have gone fishing to see who would turn up as a potential buyer. By using the code, the potential buyer could check the letters against his original message and know he was dealing with the right people. Remember this was 1948. There was no internet. No fax. No way to electronically transmit a photograph. Communication, especially between continents, was still rudimentary by today's standards."

"Why not just bring a copy of the telegram then?"

"I can't answer that for certain, but keep in mind this individual carried no identification whatsoever, and also had removed all of the labels from his clothing. We know he did this himself, because it was not just the labels on the clothes he was wearing, but also on those found in the suitcase, which the murderer did not have access to. Whatever he was up to, he took extraordinary measures to keep from being identified. One would suppose a copy of the telegram would have been a dangerous thing to carry. Also the fact that the code was written in the back of a copy of the Ruba'iyat would have served as further verification. Someone could have stolen the telegram or the police could have found it. Only the potential buyer and the seller would have known the meaning of the code."

"Well how do you know that telegram has anything to do with this book in the first place?" Megan asked.

"The truth is, I can't be one hundred percent sure of any of this, but let me tell you what I've discovered since I found the message. As I mentioned, I made the assumption the letters G.O. in the first line stands for the Great Omar. That is how everyone began to refer to the work after it was assumed lost on the Titanic. Secondly, I assumed that the letters in the last line, T.G. belonged to whoever had the book at that time. Initially, I had no clue as to his identity. All I knew was, if he had the Great

Omar, he had it illegally, and there was a high probability that he was involved in its theft and the murder of the policeman in New York City. Of course, the book may have changed hands since that theft, possibly more than once, but the chances of that happening without someone knowing about it are slim. This is one of the world's most famous lost treasures. People inevitably talk about such things, albeit very quietly. If he was not involved in the original theft, there was still a high probability he was an unscrupulous broker who had been contracted by the thieves to find a buyer. I started doing research on rare book collectors and agents from that time period. I found two possibilities with the initials T.G., and one of these was a man by the name of Theodore Granger who lived in Coral Springs, Florida at the time. On a hunch, during one of my visits to Florida, I cross-checked that name against police records and discovered that Mr. Granger was the victim of an unsolved murder in March of 1949. Potentially another death related to the Great Omar."

"Wow, this story gets creepier all the time." Megan said.

"Indeed."

Ham stood and stretched his arms and legs.

"Sorry. If I sit too long these old bones tend to complain about it. I'm almost finished but, before I go any further, let me ask if you would like to take some lunch at this point. I'm afraid I skipped my breakfast this morning and I'm a bit hungry and more than a little thirsty. We can get something light if you prefer."

"Sure." Megan said. "I'll bet you know exactly where to go, too."

"Yes. It happens I know where to find the best hot dogs in all of Charleston."

12

I had to laugh when Ham walked us over to a food truck parked on the street nearby. He seemed to enjoy our reaction.

"I'm impressed." Megan said. "If I didn't know better, I'd think you lived in Brooklyn for a while."

"No, I haven't had the pleasure." He pressed his index finger to the end of his nose. "I do, however, have a nose for good food and I was not exaggerating about the hot dogs. You will have to let me know if you agree."

We returned to our picnic table in the park and ate our lunch in relative silence.

"Wow these really are good. Almost as good as a Coney Dog, but not quite."

"I'll have to try one some day, if they are better than these."

"So, where did you find that telegram?" I asked when we were almost finished.

"I was in Miami about a month ago. One of the things I do is to attend certain high profile estate sales. My talent, if I may say so, is to locate and purchase objects of value who's true worth may be unappreciated by the current owners or the auction houses. I make a very nice income reselling these items to my client list. Occasionally I am able to ferret out an object that is of great value but has been grossly underappreciated, let us say. I started out small. Not much more than an antiques dealer so to speak. But I soon found that I have a natural eye for valuable items. Over the years as my personal worth has increased, I have been able to play the game at a much higher level. I am now able to bid on some very valuable items with my own money and on speculation that I can find a buyer for them."

"In any case, the estate I was visiting was that of a man named Eurico Alvarez. He was one of the wealthiest members of the Miami social scene. It is rumored that his great wealth was a result of certain illegal activities and the penchant of some to, as they say, powder their noses, if you catch my drift."

Megan laughed and Ham took a moment to enjoy the compliment.

"At this point I had not thought about the Great Omar for quite some time. It was always somewhere in the back of my mind but the trail had gone cold and I just assumed it was locked away in a private owners collection somewhere. Now Mr. Alvarez was a collector, primarily of pre-Columbian art. Several of the items in the estate were found to be stolen antiquities and were subsequently returned to their countries of origin. In addition, he was a collector of rare books. Especially richly bound titles from Europe and the Middle East. He had several exquisitely bound examples in display cases in his study. Quite extraordinary actually. I later bid on several items and did manage to purchase a nice Shakespeare folio which I subsequently sold. One of the things I like to bid on are collections of old correspondence and manuscripts. Most of it turns out to me of little value, but I am usually able to purchase these collections for a song, so if I occasionally find something of value it is all profit. Also, I have to admit, I enjoy the investigative work involved. In my younger years I worked as an investigator for Scotland Yard in London. The telegram turned up in one of the cartons I purchased at this estate sale. It was in a file folder with several photographs of the Great Omar."

"You were a policeman?" Megan asked with a skeptical look on her face.

"Well, a detective actually. I was not so out of shape in those days. One supposes I was hired for my brains, not my muscles. All that aside, I was intrigued by the find but I was very busy at the time with the estate sale and I had already seen Mr. Alvarez's collection and it did not include the Omar. A while later, when things had become a little more relaxed, I decided to get a fresh look at the whole mystery. I assembled all of my notes on the book along with a lot of anecdotal evidence I had collected and I just started reading everything again. It was almost two in the morning when I finally noticed the letters in the code matched the words in the telegram. It was quite a moment. It was after this discovery that I contacted Annabel Weiss."

"How old was this guy Alvarez? He must have been in his nineties if he was involved with this thing in 1948."

"A very keen observation, Mark and something I questioned as well. Mr. Alvarez was in his early sixties. It turns out, however, that he had actually inherited his fortune and, one might conjecture, his business interests from his father who was a well known bootlegger in the twenties. He had a fleet of Bimini boats bringing in rum from the Bahamas during prohibition. The acorn, as they say, does not fall very far from the tree. Apparently it was Mr. Alvarez the elder who had started the family interest in rare books. Remarkable in itself, since he was said to be unable to read English."

"So what was the man in Australia doing with the code?" Megan asked.

"The real question is who in Australia would have interest in the Great Omar. In my research I found the name of a prominent art dealer who at the time resided in Brisbane, Australia. He also had offices in Quebec, Canada and Paris, France. Anecdotal evidence suggests that this individual was not entirely scrupulous. A reasonable cause for suspicion, one would say. Unfortunately, this man passed away in the nineteen sixties so we shall likely never be able to know for sure. Far be it for me to cast aspersions upon the dead. I did discover, however, that this individual had a particular interest in rare books of poetry"

"So what do you think happened?"

"Well, at this point I don't believe the Great Omar ever ended up in Australia. That tale has all the earmarks of a deal gone terribly wrong. We probably will never know the details, and I could, of course, be wrong. But I have been operating under the supposition that the book stayed in this country and still resides here. I think it is likely that the dead man in Australia was working for or with Mr. Granger. It could be that Mr. Granger had struck a deal with Mr. Alvarez to purchase the book, but he got greedy and began fishing for another potential buyer. Perhaps he was discovered and it cost him his life. We'll never know."

"Okay. So all of that is very interesting." I said. "But where does it leave us. The book is apparently still lost, right?"

"Actually, I don't believe so. I think I know where it is. In point of fact I don't know its physical location, but I believe I know who has it."

"Who?"

"Before we get into that, I want to discuss what we will do with the book, should we be able to recover it. My agreement with Ms. Weiss was that I would sell the book to the highest bidder and I would retain my commission which would be five percent on an object of this value. We made this tentative agreement before I knew what was involved. At the time I assumed it would be a simple matter of locating the book, potentially among Mr. Alvarez's possessions, establishing Ms. Weiss's claim, and then selling it to a collector."

"How would you establish her claim?"

"Well fortunately, as I said, Ms. Weiss retained very good records including a copy of the original paperwork from the shipment from Dublin with a bill of sale. She had documented the discovery of the rare book by means of photographs taken by her mother. As well, she retained copies of the police reports surrounding the theft. Now granted, if we were forced to go into some elaborate discovery of ownership, things could get a little confused, but my guess is none of the potential claimants, if there are any, would know anything about this book. I'm relatively certain we could sufficiently defend ownership and fairly quickly. We don't have to satisfy an auction house, just the New York police department. They would not be interested in going back beyond the theft in New York. All that, however, was before Ms. Weiss passed away and before the Great Omar slipped below the radar once again. I also believe that whoever ransacked Ms. Weiss's apartment was looking for the documentation I have just described to you. Fortunately, and at my request I might add, Ms. Weiss handed this documentation over to her lawyer weeks ago."

"Why would anyone want the documentation?"

"It goes back to the ownership issue. Whoever has the book; it would be in his best interest to destroy any evidence of ownership by another party."

"How would he know about Annabel?" Megan asked.

"That part of the story is the most well documented of all. Anyone with interest in the Great Omar would have known about the theft in New York and from whom it was stolen. In any case, the thing is no longer a simple matter at all."

"So now what?" Megan asked.

"I will propose a different arrangement to the two of you, assuming, of course you produce the letter from Ms. Weiss verifying your claim."

"We have a copy with us."

"May I see it please?"

I removed the letter from the inside pocket of my jacket and handed it over to Ham. He spent some time reading the two pages and then turned them over to examine the reverse side.

"Very well. It does appear to be as you claimed."

He looked at Megan for a moment.

"Miss Weiss obviously loved you very deeply, Megan. Again, I offer you my sincere condolences. Let me reiterate that this letter, or more precisely the original letter, should be kept in a safe place. Everything that happens from here on is dependent on this document and your claim of ownership. May I hold onto this copy?"

"Sure, that's for you."

"And the original?"

"It will be in a safe deposit box until we need it."

"So then, I propose that we form a legal partnership for the purpose of recovering the book. I would have my attorney draw up paperwork to formalize our agreement. If we are successful, I will sell the book to my client in return for one third of the sale price, after expenses."

"That's pretty steep don't you think?"

"Actually I don't think so at all, Mark. You are free, if you choose to do so, to pursue this matter on your own from here on. You may attempt to find the book, take possession, and then find a buyer. In spite of my labors to date, I would not object to you taking this option nor would I inhibit your efforts in any way. All I would ask would be, should you find the book, to at least allow me to hold the book in my hands one time before it goes into someone's private collection. I make this offer because I am an honest man and do not wish to take advantage of anyone. My reputation is more valuable to me over time then the Great Omar will ever be. Secondly, I frankly believe it would be nearly impossible for you to get your hands on the book without my help. As you have seen, I have put in a great deal of time and energy pursuing the Great Omar. I feel that my efforts to date, plus the planning and execution of our attempt to recover it going forward, is worth that much. If you think about it, I'm sure you will agree."

"That's okay with me." Megan said. "I don't mind giving you a third. I think you've earned it.

But I still would like to know what we're going to have to do."

"I have some ideas we can discuss. Not all of the details have been worked out. I wanted to make sure we were in agreement before I took it any further."

"Well how much do you think you could get for it?"

"I have an offer in hand for five million dollars. I will probably be able to negotiate that up to perhaps six million."

"So what happens next?"

"Well, if we are agreed on the arrangements I have a lot of work to do. I have some obligations I must tend to first and I need to go off to the court house in Columbia at some point. How long will you be in Charleston?"

"We were intending to leave tomorrow. We'll be staying at a condo in Boca Raton for a couple of weeks."

"That actually works quite well. I need to visit Mr. Alvarez's home one more time and we can get together then. In any case, I will need at least a week, perhaps two. I suggest we keep in touch by cell phone. You already have my number, but I will need either yours, Megan or Mark's. Preferably both. I will keep you advised of any developments. Lastly, I believe it would be prudent of you not to discuss the Great Omar with anyone, even casually. I would also be suspicious of anyone expressing interest in the book for any reason."

13

The Condo in Boca Raton was on the beach just north of the Thieves Inlet. For the first couple of days, the open space and sunlight seemed to have Megan rattled. She kept moving between the beach and the condo and was spending part of the afternoon inside with the drapes drawn. Gradually the magnetic pull of the ocean got to her and she began spending more and more time on the beach. She was fair-skinned and I got her a wide brimmed beach hat and a cover-up to keep her from burning. She was sitting on a blanket with the hat tied under her chin and the brim swept back by the breeze coming in off the water. She hadn't yet lost her city face. That wary expression I remembered from our first meeting, but she did seem to be a little more relaxed each day. There was still a lot of tension in her body and that was going to take some time. I looked over and laughed at her.

"What?" She asked, grinning at me from behind her huge sunglasses.

"Nothing. You look like a lighthouse keeper. Maybe I should get you some binoculars."

"Well, that's what we're doing here right? Waiting for my ship to come in."

"Yes, but you're supposed to be relaxing too."

"That's easy for you to say. I don't think I know how to do it. I keep thinking I need to go find someplace to sleep tonight. I feel like I should be out in the park looking for people who want a cartoon done. I feel like I'm being lazy."

"Don't worry. You'll get the hang of it."

"Let's not do the beach tomorrow. Maybe we can walk downtown a little."

"Sure. In fact there's a nice little Art Museum over in Mizner Park. I think you'd like it."

"What kind of art?"

"I was only there once. I remember they had a little of everything. There were some interesting drawings and some European and

American painters. I think they have traveling exhibitions also but I don't know if anything's there right now. We'll go check it out. There's a sculpture garden out back. You could bring some of your drawings. Maybe they'd be interested."

"I doubt that. But anyway, that sounds great."

"Good. That's what we'll do then. Besides I want to take you shopping."

"You already did that."

"Yeah, but I'm in the mood for some night life. We need to get you some stepping-out clothes. A killer dress and some dancing shoes."

Megan laughed. "I didn't know you were into the Rave scene."

"The what?"

"Dancing shoes is what they call Ecstasy on the street. I'm not really into it but I will if you will."

"No, I mean heels."

"You'll have to hold me up. I can barely walk in those things."

"How hard could it be?" I said, laughing.

"I'd like to see you try it. It isn't as easy as it looks."

"Well, we'll go someplace nice in town tonight so you can practice before we do Palm Beach."

"Isn't that where the rich people hang out?"

"That's one of them."

"I'm going to feel like I'm sneaking into the movies. I don't feel like I belong in a place like that."

"Let me tell you the first secret of your new life, Megan. You are who you say you are and you belong where you want to belong. All you ever need to do is keep smiling. In fact, when we go up to Palm Beach I'm going to rent us a limo for the evening. Wait until you see how people react to you when you step out of one of those. You'd be surprised how many of those people are just out playing dress-up and going into hock to pull it off."

"You're spending way too much money on me. I want you to keep track of it all so I can pay you back."

"I don't care about the money. I came down here to relax and try to enjoy myself. I thought I was going to be alone and I wasn't sure I was even going to like it. You have no idea how much more fun it is having you here with me."

"I'm having a great time too. It's just doesn't feel right to me."

"Yeah, like I said. It's going to take time."

"No, that's not it. The whole thing just feels like some kind of mistake. I don't want to be rich. I've seen too many rich people and I really didn't like most of them. They look down their noses at everybody and they judge you by what you have instead of by who you are."

"They're not all that way. Besides you can be yourself. It doesn't have to change you."

"I think it does. I don't think you can stop it. It doesn't seem like there's any middle ground."

"Well, you can still walk away from it if you want, Megan."

"I know I can. But if I do, then what? I don't think I can go back to living the way I was. It just seemed normal to me then. I guess because I didn't have any other choice and I didn't know any other life. But the thought of going back out on the street like that just makes me sick."

"You're not going to have to go back to that, Megan. That life is over. You can stay with me for as long as you need to. I'll help you get started with something. Who knows? Maybe we could do something together. Start a small business on the side or something."

"Doing what? All I can do is draw cartoons."

"That's not all you can do by a long shot. You just haven't had the resources to explore anything else. Anybody who can make it on the streets of New York like you did has got to be full of potential. Like the song says,' if you can make it there you can make it anywhere'."

She put her arms around me and held onto me for a moment.

"You really are a good person. I can't believe how lucky I was to run into you that day."

"Oh, I don't know. I think there are a lot of people who would have offered to help you if they knew you a little. If they knew your circumstances."

"Sure, a few people would have given me a ride, but not many would have stayed with me to help me out like you did. Probably nobody else. You took a risk for me. You gave up your time and now you're looking out for me. I'll never forget that."

"You know you wouldn't have to keep all the money anyway Megan. You could buy yourself a nice place to live and a car and then put enough away to cover all of your expenses for the rest of your life. You could give the rest to charity if you wanted to. Think of how many people you could help. You could go back and visit your friends in the city and do something nice for them. It doesn't have to make you greedy. You just need to know how much is enough."

"Yeah. I thought about that. I just don't want anybody else to get hurt because of this book."

"Well, you don't have to make any decisions for a while anyway. For now you should just forget about it and have a good time."

Megan was more in her element in town. We stopped at a bank and opened a safe deposit box and then headed over to the art museum. We spent the entire morning there. She was especially intent on the drawings. Several times the security people had to ask her to step back a little because her nose was almost touching the canvas. Later, when we went shopping, she insisted that I go somewhere else for a while. She wanted to surprise me. I walked around the park which had once been an enclosed mall. I did a little shopping himself, but mostly I was trying to imagine a future that made some sense. Something that I could enjoy doing again. When I returned she was sitting in an overstuffed chair looking out the window with a sheepish grin on her face.

"I spent too much money. I'm really sorry. We can go find something cheaper. I liked the dress too much before I saw the price tag."

"If it's more than five hundred dollars I'm going to make you order corn flakes for dinner."

"Five hundred dollars? Who would spend that kind of money on a dress?"

"Pretty much any woman I've ever known, if she could get away with it."

I gave the clerk my credit card without looking at the total.

"I don't know how to thank you. I really don't."

"You need to stop worrying about that."

"Can we walk around a little before we go back?"

"Sure. Does it make you feel like you're back in the city?"

"Maybe a little. I'm used to spending a lot of time in the park. These palm trees don't give you much shade though. It doesn't look anything like New York. I guess that's why people come down here. It doesn't even look real to me."

"Is that good or bad?"

"A little of both I guess. I like it here but I don't think I could live here forever. It's just too strange."

We walked for a while and then sat on a bench in the gazebo. Megan looked genuinely happy for the first time since I met her. She actually had a smile on her face as she watched the people parading by.

"I can't believe how people dress down here. Look at that guy over there with the pink shorts. If he walked through Central Park looking like that somebody would kick his ass just for the hell of it."

I laughed. "I'm still having trouble imagining you surviving in that place. How in the world did you keep yourself safe?"

"Well, a lot of it's about attitude. If you walk around looking like a victim you get to be one sooner or later. After a while you figure out where to go and where not to go. I tried not to be out alone too much after dark or in lonely places. Especially after that creep started stalking me. Besides, I'm tougher than I look. I lived with a guy for a while who had a black belt in Aikido. He taught me some things. I'm not that good at it but I can handle myself a little. We used to spar with these wooden swords. I don't know how I'd do with a real one, but I could knock the crap out of you in a stick fight."

I laughed again.

"I'm serious. Stand up; I want to show you something."

I stood facing her.

"Now try to grab me by my top."

I reached out toward her but she grasped me by the back of my hand and then spun around tucking under my arm. She moved amazingly fast and I would have flipped over onto my back except that she eased up on me. The pain in my wrist and elbow was excruciating.

"Do you give up?"

"I surrender. Jesus that really hurt."

"I'm sorry I didn't mean to hurt you."

"Well, I guess we won't be needing a body guard. I'm impressed."

"It's like I said, that's the first thing people ask about when they find out you're homeless. But getting physically hurt is really not the big issue. It's what it does to your head that does the real damage. I know some people who have lived like that all their lives. I've seen the lines grow on their faces like they were starting to shrivel up inside. If you live like that for too long, there's no way out. You end up pushing a shopping cart around and sleeping under a bridge like a troll. I thought that was what was going to happen to me. I thought I was going to lose it some day like that guy in the fountain. I wouldn't have admitted it, but I was starting to feel desperate. I don't think I would have kept my sanity too much longer. Anyway, I don't want to think about it. Lets head back and see if we can catch the sunset."

When we got back to the condo, Megan insisted on putting on her new outfit to see if I liked it. I was sitting out on the balcony nursing a drink and staring out at the ocean when she called me in. When she emerged from the bedroom my jaw dropped. She looked ten years older. I already knew there was a beautiful young woman hidden behind the loose fitting clothes and the city attitude, but she looked stunning. It was a short, form fitting, sleeveless lace dress the color of her eyes. When I held her that night in Charleston there was nothing remotely sexual about it. Looking at her now I couldn't help but wonder why."

"What's the matter, cat got your tongue?"

"You look beautiful. You don't even look like the same person."

"I'm not. I'm somebody new. Just like you said I would be. Do you like the dress?"

"It looks great on you. I can't wait to show you off tonight."

"I'm glad you like it. I'm going to get changed now so we can walk on the beach for a little bit. Is that Okay?"

"Sure."

She started to turn but I reached out and took her by the arm.

"Wait here for a moment. I have something I want to give you."

I went into the bedroom and got the present I had bought for her earlier in the day.

"This is for you. I found it while you were shopping and I had to buy it for you."

She opened the box and a look of amazement came over her face. She turned it over and looked at the inscription on the back and then she started to cry. For a moment I thought I had done the wrong thing but then she threw her arms around me and pressed her lips against mine.

"My god. Where did you get this?"

She removed it from the box and placed it around her neck, turning to look at her reflection in the mirror. She kissed me again and then took my hand and pulled me toward the bedroom. She whispered into my ear.

"There will be another sunset tomorrow night."

We had dinner at Max's Grille. It was one of those places that had been around forever, and there was a reason for it. The food was great and there was a lively crowd at the bar. Megan seemed like a different person in a dress and heels. She was watching the other women intently as if she were learning how to act. At first she seemed a little ill at ease, but as the evening wore on she started to relax a bit. The wine helped. After we ate we moved to the outdoor lounge beneath the outsized umbrellas to have a drink and watch the crowd. It was a beautiful evening and the people out on the promenade were dressed to be noticed. Megan was in her element and I was content to watch her taking it all in.

"Did you enjoy your dinner?" I asked, after a while.

"Are you kidding? How could I not. I can count on one hand the number of times I've eaten in a place like this. Usually I can't even get in the front door. You're going to make me fat if we keep doing this."

"You've got a ways to go before you need to start worrying about that. Anyway, if you want, tomorrow we can buy some groceries and cook dinner back at the condo."

"I'm glad you said we. I can do grilled cheese but that's about it."

"I'm not much better, but we can experiment a little. If we screw it up we can always order a pizza."

"Have you thought any about what you want to do next? With your life I mean. Are you going to start a new business or something?"

"I haven't really been thinking about it much. I guess I've been busy thinking about the book."

"I'm sorry. I don't want to be getting in your way. If you want I can go out on my own tomorrow and you can take some time for yourself."

"You're not in the way. In fact, I think this is how change happens. Not by sitting around thinking about it. You have to get out in the world and start doing things. That's why I came down here in the first place. Besides, I think you're a good influence on me. You think so far out of the box you can't even see the box anymore."

She laughed. "There's a box?"

"Yeah, there's a box. It's where I've been for the past ten years. I just managed to get out of it and I don't want to jump into another one for lack of a better idea. Like you said. There's got to be more to life than just making money."

"Right, but you have to have some. Trust me. It isn't easy living without it."

"What would you do if you didn't have to worry about it, Megan? I don't mean if you get your fortune. That's a whole other discussion. Let's just say you had a comfortable place to live and enough to have some kind of normal life. What would you do?"

"I don't know, really. I guess I feel best when I'm helping people. Like you said, it gets you out of your head. It makes you feel like you have some kind of purpose. I'd really like to take art lessons again too, and have the money to see it through this time."

I started to reply when his cell phone rang.

"Hello?"

"Hello Walt."

"I'm down here in Boca. At the condo. Where are you?"

"Are you on your way back?"

"What's going on with you? Jennifer is scared out of her mind."

I listened without speaking. He was being evasive. Like he was afraid to talk over the phone.

"All right. Yeah I know where Homestead is."

"Tomorrow night? No I don't know the place but I'll find it. What time?"

"Okay. I'll see you at eight."

I hung up the phone and looked over at Megan.

"That was Walt. He wants to meet tomorrow night. How would you feel about spending the evening by yourself at the condo while I meet him?"

"Sure. I don't mind. What's going on?"

"He didn't want to talk about it over the phone. He sounds pretty worried and I think it would be better if I went alone."

14

The bar was in what looked like an abandoned warehouse in a seedy section of the city out by the Air Force base. There was a forlorn, neon sign above the door identifying the place as Rick's Tavern, but the neon R had ceased to function and was not likely to ever glow again. The locals apparently had long ago christened the place ick's. The Country and Western music hit me like a wave as I opened the door and stepped inside. It was so dark I had to wait for a few moments to allow my eyes to adjust. It smelled like Sunday morning at a Frat house. A handful of hardcore drinkers were slumped over their beers, but the place was still mostly empty. I spotted Walt down at the end of the bar. The soles of my shoes stuck to the beer drenched linoleum as I made my way down the row of barstools. Walt stood up and threw his arms around me, patting me on the back. His smile was fleeting and I could see the worry on his face. He had lost a lot of weight and his eyes looked like he needed a good night's sleep.

"Hello, Mark. It's good to see you, man. Thanks for coming."

He picked up his beer and we moved to a booth at the back near the emergency exit. The waitress came over and stood glaring at us in silence. She looked to be in her forties and was dressed in a cowgirl blouse and boots, and a short black skirt that might have looked good on a woman half her age. There were full sleeve tattoos on both of her arms and something cryptic written on her neck in faded blue cursive. Her hair was the color of black shoe polish. She looked at me. Her face immobile.

"I'll have what he's drinking, and bring him another one too, please."

She nodded and walked back to the bar.

"Jesus, how long has it been? Three years or something. I've lost track. You look great."

"About that. It's good to see you too but what the hell is going on, Walt? You look like hell and Jen is worried sick about you. She doesn't know what to tell the kids."

"I know she is. Believe me I don't want to be here either, but it had to be done. I got myself into some real trouble. If I hadn't left when I did, I don't think I would have made it?"

"What are you talking about?"

"I'm in rehab, Mark."

"Rehab? For what?"

"Heroin."

"Come on man." I said, half laughing. "I'm serious."

"I'm serious too."

I just stared at him. It took a while for me to get my head around it.

"What happened? I don't understand."

"It's complicated." He stared down at the table. "I went over the edge, Mark. I didn't believe it could ever happen to me. I thought I was too strong. I was wrong."

"Are you using now."

Walt looked me in the eye.

"No, no. I'm clean. That's why I came down here. The rehab is working but it isn't pretty. The first couple of weeks I was in detox. They wouldn't even let me out of the place. It was like I was in jail and I was really sick. I couldn't have gone through it in front of Jennifer and the kids. I was praying she wouldn't find out. I feel like crap."

He took a sip of his beer and his hands were shaking as he put the glass back down on the table. He didn't even look like the same person I had known all those years. I was beyond shocked and I didn't know how to react. He was just looking down into his beer and suddenly I just felt sorry for him.

"How could you let this happen, Walt?"

"I ask myself the same question every day, and I don't really know how. I thought I was on my way to making it big. Looking back, the signs were all there. I just ignored them until I was in over my head. It all started after I left Oracle. Do you remember Charlie Lake? I think you met him once."

"Vaguely."

"He left Oracle about a year and a half ago to form a new start-up called CIC. Cyber Infometrics Corporation. Charlie was always big into the stock market and he got tired of spending his time developing business enterprise software. CIC develops trading algorithms for the stock market. He eventually offered me a position with an equity stake. It was a little out of my comfort zone but I figured it was now or never. It's big business Mark. I was pretty happy at Oracle and I was moving up the ladder but you know how it goes. There are only so many seats at the big table and I didn't have the pedigree to get there. CIC was the brass ring. It was a chance to break away from the nine to five slave collar and to make a fortune. To have Jennifer and the kids set for life. I couldn't turn it down."

"What were you working on?"

"Well, how much do you know about the stock market?"

"Not that much really. Other than my 401K seems to be making more money for my broker than for me. I have a basic understanding about how trades work. I know what most people know."

"Well, you can pretty much forget all that. Most of the trades today aren't even made by human beings, they're made by computers. I'm talking about more than 50% of the volume on

221

any given trading day and that number keeps rising."

"So you write programs to execute trades?"

"Well, no. That's what developers were doing three or four years ago. It was a race to develop the best algorithm. Software that would squeeze the last penny out of all of the market volatility on a given day. Making trades in micro-seconds, usually in the last few minutes before the markets closed. They call it black-box trading. The profits from any one transaction are small, which is why the individual investor can't play the game. The computer can make millions of small trades, each of which yields only a tiny profit, but the cumulative effect is big bucks."

"Yeah. I've read a few articles about that."

"Well, it's gone way beyond simple trading programs. You know the markets move continuously, based on financial information released by corporations during the course of the day. Financial information like earnings, stock buy-backs, inventory levels, new product releases, that sort of thing. Even news from other companies that are not even obviously related. It's very involved. Very technical. It was always the analyst's job to interpret that information and decide what bearing it would have on the stock price. The amount of information they had to sort through was staggering. So the software developers moved one step back and started writing programs that would automatically collect and organize that kind of information, and feed it to the people who were executing the trades. It was the next evolution of trading and the software developers were in a war again to see who could come up with the most effective algorithm. The thing is, having a good algorithm is only part of the challenge. It helps you drill down into the data, but somebody still has to figure out whether the information would have a positive or negative effect on the stock price, and how large an effect it would be. There was still a human being in the loop. So that created the new game in town."

"Which is what?"

"Which is developing an algorithm that would continuously scan the net for business news, interpret what effect it would likely have on the price of any given stock, and then feed that information directly into the trading program. The algorithm was no longer just providing raw data. It was making a decision as to what the news meant and acting on it. All without human intervention."

"That all sounds a little ominous to me."

"Yeah, well it has already caused some problems. You may remember what they called the Flash Crash back in May of 2010. The Dow lost more than 600 points and then suddenly recovered before the end of trading. It was the second largest point swing in the history of the exchange. All because of a software problem. In the long run I don't think it's a good thing but if you're going to take advantage of it, this is the time. Things have gotten really cloak and dagger. Now there are these things called Dark Pools that do trades outside of the traditional markets. A lot of their orders are what they call 'iceberged', which means a really large trade is broken into a series of smaller trades to disguise the magnitude of the transaction. There are what are called 'gamers' or 'sharks' who ping the trades to see if they are cumulatively significant. It's the Wild West all over again. The SEC and the CFTC are looking at it very closely. For now though, there is a pot of gold out there for the taking. We went for it."

"Okay. I get all that. It still doesn't tell me what happened to you."

"We were in over our heads, Mark. To begin with, developing these programs is difficult because you need to analyze the effects of certain kinds of information over historically long periods of time and with a ton of variables. It would take a hundred years to do that with a normal processor. It has to be simulated on a supercomputer."

"You have a supercomputer?"

"In my dreams. No, but we are able to rent time on one called Vulcan at Lawrence Livermore Labs. It's not as fast as the one they use to simulate nuclear detonations, but it's plenty fast enough for what we need. It can do something like five quadrillion calculations per second. Five petaflops. The thing is it's not cheap. It costs nearly two thousand dollars an hour and to do what we were attempting, well, we were burning through money like it was tinder. There came a point where I had to decide to either go all in or to walk away. We were really close. It's difficult to evaluate but as far as we could see our accuracy rate was off the charts. I decided to roll the dice. I borrowed everything I could on the house. Liquidated nearly every asset I had. Charlie had already done the same."

"And then what?"

"It wasn't enough. We were still short on operating capital and I was actually thinking about throwing in the towel. I would have taken a big loss but with my skill set, I figured I could get a well paying position pretty easily. There are still companies that actually value a guy who's willing to take a few risks these days. Instead of playing it safe all the time. It's an entrepreneurial market out there. I wasn't really worried about it. I was ready to start over."

"So why didn't you?"

"Well, Charlie suddenly came up with some cash. Enough, we thought, to get us over the hump. He was vague about where he got it. He said it was from an investor that wanted a piece of the company if we succeeded. I was a little put out that he wasn't more open about it, but it was Charlie's company. I have an equity stake but he was always going to call the shots. I really wasn't concerned about the management structure anyway. Our intent was always to sell our algorithm to the highest bidder on an exclusive basis and then liquidate the company and walk away with the money."

"So what happened?"

"We got beat. It's as simple as that. In retrospect it was crazy to think we could win against some of the corporate muscle that was in the game. The ironic thing is we had built a better program. Measurably better. We just weren't able to handle the liability issues. With trading companies exposed to millions in losses they had no interest in doing business with a green startup with no assets they could sue us against. We lost."

"Is that why you started doing dope?"

"No. It happened way before that. You can't imagine the pressure when you have everything you own in the game. I was working late hours, bringing work home. It was making me physically sick. Sometimes the tension was so bad I had to go into the men's room and puke. I thought I was going to have a heart attack. There was this young analyst named Karen that Charlie hired. She was a little wild, but she was really good and she worked hard. She would even stay after hours to help. I caught her snorting it one night. I thought it was coke. She begged me not to tell Charlie and I didn't. I didn't really care what she did as long as she was doing a good job. It got to be a little conspiracy we had going."

"Were you cheating on Jen?"

"No, not then, not at first. It wasn't like that. I love Jen. I didn't have any interest Karen that way, but one night I was so wired I was physically shaking. She offered me a line and I

227

did it. Just a little bit. It changed everything. With the tension gone I was able to think clearer. I wrote a couple of sub-routines that Charlie thought were brilliant. I actually felt better than I had in months. It got to be a regular thing. A couple of nights a week she would stay late and we'd do a line. It wasn't like I had to have it or anything. It was like medicine. One night she forgot to bring it in and she invited me back to her apartment to do a line before I went home. One thing lead to another. A couple of weeks after that we both started to get sick. That's when I started shooting up. I knew I was on a bad road, but I didn't know how to stop. I knew if I didn't stop I was going to die."

"So what happened?"

"One night, Karen overdosed. I was over at her place and she shot up first. I saw her go under and I was scarred to death. She stopped breathing. I called 911 and started giving her CPR. The EMTs carry this auto injector now with a drug called Naloxone and that brought her around. That was my wake-up call. I started looking for someplace to go into rehab. Someplace where Jen and the kids wouldn't have to see it. It needed to be somewhere I could stay for a few weeks at least. Karen knew some people in Key Largo who agreed to let me stay for a while. I just got out a few days ago."

"Is she down here with you?

"Not at first. She came down about two weeks ago. We're going to meetings together. It helps, having someone who understands what you're going through. I don't know if I could do it alone."

"So are you recovered now?"

"I don't know. I know I never want to do it again, but that's now. They say you're never really free of it. All I want is to go back to Jen, if she'll have me. To hug my kids again. To have a normal life with a normal job."

"So why don't you?"

"Because we're still in trouble. I found out Charlie had gone out on the street to get the cash. He's a confident guy and I guess he thought it would put us over the top and there would be no problem paying it off."

"What do you mean by out on the street? You went to a loan shark?"

"Not me. I wouldn't have done that. But Charlie did, without telling me. At this level they don't call themselves loan sharks, but yeah, that's what he did. They're called Unregistered Finders, and the practice is illegal if you're not registered with the SEC, except for a few 'safe harbor' exemptions. Charlie tried every legitimate avenue to raise capital. Venture capital firms, angel investors, even crowd sourcing. Nobody would bite. Like I said, I was ready to walk away before he came up with the money. I had no idea it was something illegal."

"And now he can't pay up?"

"Well, when we found out this unregistered finder was operating illegally, Charlie refused to pay his fee. That's when we found out where the money really came from. It came from some big drug supplier out of Charlotte. Apparently it was all part of a money laundering scheme. The money Charlie got was in cash. Very dirty cash. He swears he didn't know. They kept the transactions in amounts less than ten thousand dollars so the banks wouldn't have to report it. That part he knew about. We stood to make millions on this, Mark. That kind of money can blind a man."

"Jesus Christ, Walt. How could you let this happen?"

"I just told you how. I screwed up big time. At this point I'm not even sure I can ever make it right again."

"Well what are you going to do?"

"I'm buying time. Charlie was the one who negotiated the deal but they know about me and as far as they're concerned I owe the money just like Charlie does. If they come to talk to me, I don't want it to be at my house in front of Jen and the kids. That's the other reason I decided to leave for a while. To see if I could figure out what to do from here. Besides, I'm holding a copy of the source code. There's a possibility that if this all goes bad before Charlie can make a deal, the Feds could subpoena everything, including me. If they don't know where I am, they can't serve me. If they suspect we built the program with drug money they could take the whole thing. They could take everything."

"You've got a copy of the program?"

Walt reached into his pocket and dropped a thumb drive on the table.

"Yeah. It's on this flash drive. It's compressed and encrypted of course. That's the other reason I wanted to talk to you. I'd like to ask you to hold onto it for a little while."

"Whoa. Listen Walt, I'd like to help you but there's no way I'm going to get into some kind of mess over this. I won't do it. Why don't you just put it in a safe deposit box down here somewhere?"

"I thought about that, but that would create a record. If this all goes south, this may be the only bargaining chip I have. If it's subpoenaed, I think they could get their hands on it pretty easily unless I don't have it anymore."

"This can't be the only copy."

"No. Charlie has a copy and we've stashed enough critical code to reconstruct it if we had to. It's encrypted and hidden in the hard drives of a number of public computers that are not connected to the company. It would be a real pain in the ass, but we could do it. This copy is insurance for me. These people Charlie is dealing with think it's a machine to print money. Charlie must have done a real sales job on them. They want the program more than they want the cash. If I run out of options I'll just give it to them to pay off the debt. In the mean time, Charlie is trying to come up with the cash. He's shopping our concept around to some of our competitors to see if he can sell it. It wouldn't be a mega-deal but hopefully it would be enough to pay back what we owe and make us whole. Maybe even turn a modest profit."

"So how long are you going to have to stay down here?"

"Not too much longer, I hope. Charlie has scheduled some meetings next week. We're hoping to have a deal done by the end of the month."

"What are you doing for cash? Jen said you've been sending her money."

"Yeah. I had accumulated quite a few shares of Oracle stock before I left and I held onto some of it as a last resort. I've been selling it off a little at a time to pay the bills. It's starting to get a little thin, but hopefully we'll have this put to bed before it's gone completely."

The waitress came over and we ordered a couple of more beers. There was an awkward silence punctuated by some loud laughter coming from a bunch of guys at the bar wearing baseball uniforms. After the waitress returned with the drinks, I reached across the table and took Walt by the arm.

"Look, Walt. I've got some money stashed away from my business. If you get to where you can't pay the bills, let me know. I'll help if I can. What I won't do is pay for your habit. If you need some cash, I'll send it to Jennifer directly. Do you understand me?"

"Yeah, I do. I hope it doesn't come to that. I guess this is where you find out who your real friends are. I'm not going back to that life. I'd kill myself first."

"Don't talk like that."

"I mean it Mark. I'm not going back."

"Okay look, I'll hold onto the flash drive for you but if the cops come asking for it I'm turning it over to them. Do you understand?"

"Yeah, that's fine. The last thing I want to do is get you mixed up in this thing. Believe me."

"Is there anything I can do for you right now?"

"Yeah, there is. I hate to ask you to do this but do you think you could talk to Jen. I would do it myself but I think right now the less she knows about the whole thing the better. I just want her to know that I'm coming home as soon as I can. She doesn't deserve what I've put her through. I know that. All I can do is try to make it right."

"I don't know how to tell her what's going on with you Walt, without telling her what's going on. She's going to want to know what you're doing down here."

"Just tell her I'm in some negotiations with a potential buyer. Running tests or something. Just please don't tell her about the drugs or about Karen. That thing with Karen was just the drugs. It wasn't like I was in love with her or anything. We only did it a couple of times. It wasn't about the sex. It was about getting fixed. I'm going to come clean about that after I get through this financial mess. I don't want to lay all of this on her at once. It would be too much for her to take. Just tell her that I'm okay. Tell her it should all be wrapped up in a couple of weeks. And Mark, tell her I love her and I'm sorry for putting her through all this."

15

Megan was asleep when I got in. She was sprawled across the bed clutching her sketch book to her chest like a stuffed animal. I watched her for a moment as whatever dream she was immersed in rippled across the fine muscles of her face. I wondered what world she was in and if she was alone there too. I carefully slid the book out from under her clasped arms and then pulled the sheet up and tucked it under her chin. I turned the light off and started to undress in the dark. As I was about to lie down she stirred.

"You're back." She said, groggily. "What time is it?"

"Almost one o'clock. I'm sorry I woke you."

"No, that's okay. I was waiting up for you. So what happened?"

"I'll tell you in the morning."

"No. I've been dying to know all night. Unless you're too tired or something."

"Okay. But if we're going to be up for a while I'm going to have something to drink. Do you want anything?"

"Just some water maybe. Do you want to go out on the balcony? I was out there earlier and it's really nice. It made me feel lonely though, so I came back in."

The moon was hanging just above the horizon. It cast a ribbon of light out across the dark, still waters and straight up to our balcony like a corridor to a different universe. She pointed up at it.

"We used to lie out in the park on blankets at night when the moon was full like that. We'd pretend it was God finding us in the night with his huge flashlight. When you got caught in the beam, you had to make a confession. Then everyone had to tell a secret from their past. Something they didn't want to tell."

"And did they?"

"Yeah. Everybody told something. I think a lot of it was crap, but not all of it. It makes you feel closer to people when they unload like that. I think it makes them feel better too. Like you're not the only one with a totally screwed up life. It was fun anyway. So, tell me what your friend said."

She remained silent while I told her Walt's story, but her eyes were moving constantly across my face. It was her way, I had learned, of discovering what the words meant to me. How I felt about it inside. When I had finished she waited in silence for a moment and then she shook her head.

"I don't get it."

"You don't get what?"

"I mean that's exactly what I've been trying to say to you. They have it all don't they? I mean, they have it all right now. A beautiful house, great kids, a good job, money in the bank, all of it. And then he goes and gambles it away. For what. What else do they need? Why would he risk that? Do you understand it?"

"In a way. I mean, I wouldn't have taken that kind of risk myself. Not if I had a wife and kids depending on me. He was just looking for a way to make it to the top."

"To the top of what?"

"To be a success. I guess it's what competitive people do, if they have any ambition. I guess there's a little of it in all of us, really. At some point in your life you find yourself in a career or an occupation or you discover you have some talent. It's natural to want to be the best."

"Maybe. But it doesn't sound like your friend was trying to be the best at anything. He was just trying to make a fortune."

"Well, that's part of it. There has to be something to motivate you. I guess if you're a scientist you want the Nobel Prize. If you're in business, you want to make a pile of money."

"So do you think that's why I don't have anything? Because I don't have any ambition."

"No. I wasn't talking about you."

"No, you were talking about the real people. The people on your side of the wall."

"Look. I'm sorry Megan. I didn't mean to insult you. You should know that about me by now. This isn't about me making judgments."

"No, but you see it, don't you? You see there's something fucked up about how people like your friend look at the world. How they don't really care if they hurt other people to get what they want. Why can't they just live and be happy. That's what we do. Why isn't it enough? Isn't that why the stock market crashed anyway? Everybody was out to make their own fortune and nobody cared about doing what was right for the country. I mean, I don't know anything about the stock market but I thought it was supposed to be a way that ordinary people could share in the profits of the big corporations. Now it sounds like it's just a big game for rich people. Like playing craps or something. Playing with other people's money."

"He does care."

"Not enough. Look what he's done to his family now. He had to know he was risking everything. If he really loved them he would have walked away."

"Walt has always been a confident guy. I really don't think he realized he was in trouble until it all fell in on him."

"When you start using Heroin, that's a clue."

"You're right. Maybe it's because most of us never get a chance at having that kind of success, no matter where we come from. I don't blame Walt for taking a shot. I blame him for not knowing when to walk away."

"I'm sorry. I don't mean to be a jerk. It just comes out some times."

"It's okay. I get it. Anyway you may soon find yourself on the other side of that wall you're always talking about. Have you thought about that? Can you imagine how your life will change? I'd like to have this conversation with you after you've been there for a while."

"It won't change my life."

"How could it not?"

"Because I'm not supposed to have that kind of a life."

"How could you know that? Remember when you told me you thought bad things happen to us when we're afraid. How reality is just some agreement we have with one another. Maybe you think your life can't change and that's why it never has. Maybe what you believe is holding you back."

She looked at me then with an expression I hadn't seen from her before. As if I had opened some new door for her. Like for the first time I was present in her world, not just looking at her from the other side.

"I understand what you're saying." She said finally. "And maybe there's some truth to it. I just don't believe I'll ever be rich. That's not what my life is for."

We were quiet for a while then, just staring out over the ocean. I was tired and I didn't have the energy to challenge her. Still, I didn't want to just end the conversation with something like that hanging in the air. I was still shook up about what Walt had gotten himself into and it was hard to concentrate on anything else. I also knew the foundation of Megan's world was shaking under her feet, and she was having trouble with it. I didn't really know how to reassure her. I just changed the subject.

"I still can't figure out how he could let himself get addicted. I can't imagine him using a needle."

"I'm sure he never thought he would either. It almost never starts that way. I know a lot of people who are addicted. After that Wall St. crash a few years ago I started seeing all of these grillers showing up on the street, trying to score some dope. Most of them started with prescription drugs like OxyContin or Vicodin.

They start using Heroin because it's cheaper and you can get a better high from it. Almost all of them started by smoking or snorting it. They call it 'chasing the dragon'. They say only about a quarter of them ever get addicted but the ones that do don't last very long. They aren't able to survive in my world. It's safer to smoke it because you can control how much you inhale and you'll probably pass out before you overdose anyway. Snorting it is more dangerous but you still have some control. If you main-line it you get the whole dose and there's no way to know how much it's been cut. Let alone what it was cut with. That's why so many people O.D. That and because they develop a tolerance to it and need more all the time to get high."

"So what makes them start shooting up then?"

"Some people go for weeks, even months smoking it without getting addicted. You'd be amazed at how many of the suits in the city do it for fun. To relieve the pressure or whatever. Like your friend. Sooner or later, though, they get sick. They wake up with what feels like the flu except the only cure is more heroin. At that point it starts to take over your life. When you're junk sick, all you can think about is getting fixed. Smoking it takes some work and it's harder to get off. The needle is the fastest way. By the time you start shooting up; you don't care anymore about anything else. Your job, your family your health. Not even the fear of dying from it."

"I'm sorry to ask this, Megan, but did you ever use it?"

"No I never did, but like I said, I know a lot of people who do. I helped some of them go through withdrawal. Some of them didn't make it."

"Well, I give you a lot of credit, considering what you've been going through. You must have been tempted."

"I've been offered it dozens of times. In the first place, I never wanted to stick a needle in my arm. It just seems like a sick thing to do. I knew if I started smoking it, that's what would happen sooner or later. Besides, I guess I've never been much into escaping. I've always been more into trying to make things better. I mean, I smoke a little weed now and then just to relax and turn on my creative side, but that's different. It's like having a beer or some wine. If you escape, it's only for a little while. You have to come back to your life sooner or later, and it just keeps getting worse. Unless you don't wake up. It's never been so bad for me that I wanted to check out. I think some people who use it just have a death wish."

"I don't think Walt wants that either. At least I hope not. He really is down on himself, though. He wants me to talk to Jennifer. Let her know what's going on. Except he doesn't want me to tell her about the drugs."

"Are you going to?"

"I told him I would, but I don't want to lie to Jen either. I don't know what to do."

"I think you should tell her anyway."

"Why?"

"Because, what if he doesn't make it? What if he has an overdose and dies? How are you going to explain that to her?"

"But he quit."

"He quit for now, but he's going to be an addict for the rest of his life. Some part of him is always going to want to shoot up. If he does it again after being off it for a while, his chances of an overdose are a lot higher. His body will lose its tolerance. I don't know your friend, but from what you told me so far, he doesn't seem like somebody who'll be able to stay away when things get rough. It sounds like he's going to go through some real pain before it gets better."

"So, you think I should tell her he was having an affair too? I can't do that."

"No, that's between him and Jennifer. But an affair probably isn't going to kill him. The heroin might."

"What could she do about it anyway? I think it would just make things worse for her. He's going through rehab. She probably wouldn't want the kids to see their father that way. I think it would be better if he got himself cleaned up and then told her everything himself. Face to face."

"Well you have to tell her something."

"I know. I think I'll just tell her about the financial mess he got himself into and leave it at that."

"Are you going to see him again?"

"I'll have to at some point. He gave me a flash drive to hold for him. It's like an insurance policy he said. Sooner or later he is going to want it back."

"What happens if his friend can't get the money? What's he going to do then?"

"I don't know, Megan.   I hope it doesn't come to that."

16

As we were on our way out to get breakfast the next morning my cell phone rang. It was Ham. He didn't have time to talk but he asked if we could meet him for dinner down in Ft. Lauderdale that evening. We spent the rest of the day by the pool, but Megan seemed restless. I think in the days since our first meeting with Ham, she had managed to avoid thinking too much about the book and what changes it would bring to her life. She was living in that quiet interval between a past she was leaving behind and a future still beyond imagination. I think she sensed that was all about to change. For my part, the conversation with Walt had really shaken me. Just the idea that he could fall so far so fast was almost too much for me to comprehend. Trying to figure out how he was going to make it right was beyond me. I kept thinking about Jennifer and what I was going to tell her. How can you tell somebody you care about, that her husband has gone off the rails like that? How could I even talk to her about it without mentioning the drugs? I didn't know what to do. It was an endless conversation echoing in the back of my mind and it was making me uneasy.

Ham was staying at the Marriott Harbor Beach. I asked Megan to pack a change of clothes just in case we had to stay the night. We drove down late in the day and found him out on the patio. It was a beautiful evening. Megan was transfixed by the moment and she couldn't stop herself from staring out at the horizon. The ocean had turned that deep, almost iridescent turquoise blue that happens near sunset. In spite of the serenity of the moment, I could see she was troubled. I didn't know how to help her. Ham, in contrast to our earlier meetings, was all business and he wanted to get right to the point.

"So let me tie up some loose ends for you and tell you what has transpired since our last visit. You'll remember I was involved in the evaluation of the late Mr. Alvarez's art collection. I actually had a chance to visit his home prior to the estate sale. I had been called in by the estate lawyers as an expert to help them assess the value and authenticity of certain prominent objects prior to sending them off to the auctioneer. The auction houses have people available to do this but it is not uncommon to have an independent assessment made, just to keep everyone honest, and to avoid potentially costly under-valuations. I do this kind of consulting frequently; it creates another stream of income for me. As I mentioned to you before, Mr. Alvarez had a number of display cases containing very valuable works of art. Some of these were small sculptures, some pottery examples, and some rare books. The rare books were all resting on ornate, teak book rests. I noticed at the time that one of these cases was empty; however the book rest was still there. Obviously, a book had been removed from the collection, and rather hurriedly by the looks of things. Now, each of these display cases also had a brass identification tag at its base providing a brief description of the object. There was no tag on the empty case but there were signs that one had been recently removed. I didn't think too much about any of this at the time because this was before I found the telegram. I had no reason to believe the Great Omar would be found in this collection. It wasn't until I began looking through the loose files and manuscripts I had purchased that I had occasion to change my opinion. You see, one of the files contained a photograph of a rare Yaxchilan Lintel that was displayed in one of the cases."

"A what?" Megan asked.

Ham removed an envelope from his pocket. He opened it, and took out a three by five inch photograph. He slid it across the table so that Megan could examine it. I leaned over to get a better look.

"Yaxchilan was a Mayan city. It was located on the Usumacinta River in what now is the Mexican state of Chiapas. A lintel in this case is not a structural member; it is a decorative stone relief that is placed above a doorway or entrance to an important, usually ceremonial place. This, by the way, was confiscated and returned to the Mexican authorities when it was proven to be a stolen artifact. Now if you look closely at the photograph on the right hand side you will see another display case in the background. This one appears to contain a book of some kind. It is difficult to tell because the camera flash has been reflected off the glass. Note, however that there is a pronounced gold colored quality of the reflected light. What you can partially make out is the brass plaque at the base of the case. If you look carefully you can almost see the large lettering that gives the title of the work. On a hunch, I had this photograph analyzed by an old friend at Scotland Yard and he confirmed that the title line of the plaque is 'The Great Omar'. To say the least, I was stunned."

We looked at the photograph, squinting to try to read the inscription.

Megan looked up at Ham.

"Well that's cool, but it only tells you the Great Omar used to be in the display case. How do you know where it is now?"

"That, my dear, took a bit of additional detective work. Because stolen artifacts had been discovered, Mr. Alvarez's house suddenly became a crime scene. The police were called in and they did an inventory of every piece of art on the property. I helped them with the identification of several of the objects. All of the stolen articles were located in the study which was access controlled by means of a fairly sophisticated entry and alarm system. Mr. Alvarez's private secretary provided the police with a list of everyone who had access to the room. In addition to Mr. Alvarez and herself, there were his business manager and a third party whose name is Thomas Wesley. He was apparently in Mr. Alvarez's employ as a consultant. As it turns out, Mr. Wesley is known to me. I have seen him at several art auctions, and, although he has so far escaped the long arm of the law, he is one of those individuals who are regarded as less than scrupulous in the business. Of course Mr. Wesley was questioned by the police and claimed no knowledge that any of the artifacts were stolen. Moreover, there was evidence to show that all of the stolen objects had been owned by the original Mr. Alvarez and had been in house for many years before Mr. Wesley was involved. The police could not prove any wrongdoing, so he was eventually dropped as a suspect."

"What about the book?" Megan asked.

"Well, you see my dear; the subject of the Great Omar never came up because it was no longer present in the house. There were questions asked about the empty display case but Mr. Wesley claimed it had lately contained a rare edition of some John Donne essays. He was able to produce records showing such a book had been legitimately sold to another collector a few months prior to the death of Mr. Alvarez."

"So this guy Wesley has the book?"

"That is my inescapable conclusion."

"Couldn't it have been the secretary or the business manager?" Megan asked.

"It certainly is possible, but they were interviewed extensively by the police and both were also cleared of any suspicion. I am convinced that neither of them would have the slightest idea of the true value of the Great Omar or what to do with it. The secretary is, by all accounts an honest person who was not involved in any of Mr. Alvarez's businesses, but possibly had a close personal relationship with him, in a manner of speaking. The business manager is apparently a bit of a thug, no doubt more familiar with a gun or knife then with a rare book of poetry. He would not be able to sell the book without a lot of help."

"Well, it doesn't seem there is any evidence to prove anyone took it."

"That is still unfortunately the case, Mark. But, please, allow me to continue before you make a judgment. You see after the estate sale, I witnessed a conversation between Mr. Wesley and someone I had not seen for many years. He is originally from Iran, but he is now a British citizen. He is a prominent Art dealer with offices in New York City. His name is Daoud Ali Alfarsi. He has been questioned, although never implicated in several notorious art thefts. He is actually suspected of being the mastermind behind the theft in 1990 at the Isabella Stewart Gardner Museum in Boston. Perhaps you have heard of it. It involved the shocking loss of one of Rembrandt's most famous works, 'Storm on the

Sea of Galilee'. Also of a prominent Vermeer titled 'The Concert'. Mr. Alfarsi is rumored to be a very dangerous man and intelligent enough to stay out of prison, at least so far. Maybe it was just my policeman's intuition, but I believe there was something underhanded going on. It was quite intense and to my eye looked like some sort of negotiation. Mr. Wesley looked extremely unhappy and it was obvious he was under a lot of stress. It could have been about anything, but I have been a part of many legitimate negotiations and this had a very different feel to it. I am convinced Wesley is trying to sell the Omar."

"So where does that leave us?"

"Well, it would appear we don't have a lot of time. If the negotiation I witnessed results in a sale to Mr. Alfarsi, we will probably not see the Great Omar again. My guess is that Mr. Alfarsi made a very low-ball offer to Mr. Wesley, knowing as we do, that the book does not belong to him. On the other hand, I'm sure Wesley will hold out for the best price he can get, which may be to our advantage."

"I thought you said you didn't want to buy the book from Wesley." Megan said.

"I do not. However, if the rumors are true, it is not above Mr. Alfarsi to threaten harm to a party who refuses to sell. Especially someone with Mr. Wesley's dubious past. It's very possible the only reason Mr. Wesley is still unharmed is that Mr. Alfarsi does not know where the book is and believes his chances of finding it are not good. Mr. Wesley may be in fear for his life, and with good reason."

"So how does that help us?"

"Well. I believe we can offer Mr. Wesley both a carrot and a stick as they say. During my work at Mr. Alvarez's estate I became quite good friends with a detective from the Miami Beach police department. There are a great number of thefts from the large estates in southern Florida and a lot of them involve valuable works of art. The detective's name is David Benjamin. He leads a task force whose mission it is to track and hopefully recover such items. You do not find these things in pawn shops, as you might a stolen watch or silverware. You need to be tied into the international art and antiquities market. Detective Benjamin was very grateful for my expertise in sorting out Mr. Alvarez's estate, and offered any future assistance he could provide me. I have not discussed the Omar with him but I'm sure if I laid out the evidence I have gathered for him he would at least agree to bring Mr. Wesley in for questioning. If Wesley becomes nervous enough, he may be willing to turn the book over to the police with no questions asked for a nice finder's fee. Let us say, something on the order of one hundred thousand dollars. I didn't think you would object to such an agreement if it meant getting the Omar. Am I correct in assuming that, Megan?"

"Sure, but do you think he would go for it?"

"I suppose that depends on how much Mr. Wesley is willing to gamble with his well being. I think there is a better than even chance he would cooperate. Suppose you had found something of great value and a very dangerous person wanted it and knew you had it. An offer to turn it in to the police in exchange for a nice reward would no doubt seem attractive to you. Would it not?"

"I guess."

"So what now?" I asked.

"Well, that is why I asked to meet with you both tonight. I have an idea as to how we could proceed, but I wanted to run it by you."

257

"What do you want to do?"

"I would like to talk to my detective friend and lay my evidence out for him as I mentioned, even though there is not enough there to implicate Mr. Wesley. As I said, if he is as frightened as I think he may be, he could crumble and give the Omar to us for the reward. On the other hand, if he has his wits about him, he may demand legal representation and we would not be able to proceed further. To make that outcome less likely, before I engage detective Benjamin, I would like to see if Mr. Wesley will tip his hand to us, so to speak. To do that, I would propose using a tactic we employed often at Scotland Yard. It would require some help from the both of you."

"What tactic?" Megan asked.

"We learned over the years that a thief would sometimes lead us directly to a stolen item just by making him think we had evidence that he stole the thing. We would bring him in for questioning, and imply we knew more than we did. We would keep the interrogation relaxed so as to not unduly alarm him. The idea was to make the suspect nervous enough that he would try to move the stolen goods to a different location. After we released him, we would put a surveillance team on him to see where he went. On several occasions we were able to catch a perpetrator red-handed, trying to move the stolen goods to a safer location. Now, the police will not assign a surveillance team to a case with the kind of scant evidence we have. But the two of you could do it, if you agree. What I propose is that I contact Mr. Wesley myself and suggest a meeting between the two of us."

"Why would he do that?"

"Well he has no reason to think I know anything about or have any interest in the Omar. He only knows that I have an impressive client list and that I deal in very valuable items of art. It would be very much in his self interest to form an association with me. Who knows? He may even offer the Omar to me, although I doubt he would be that foolish. I would imply that I had a very lucrative business arrangement in mind. Once we sat down I would bring up the Omar and hopefully get his knees to knocking a bit."

"Do you know how to find him?"

"Yes. I was given Mr. Wesley's address and telephone exchange by detective Benjamin. I would call Wesley and propose a meeting at his house or a location of his choosing. The two of you would follow me and then after I leave you could 'pin a tail on him' as they say. Of course, it may not work, in which case I will contact detective Benjamin and ask him to bring Wesley in for questioning anyway."

"I don't know Ham. I don't want to put Megan in any danger here. How do you feel about it, Megan?"

"Sure. I'll do it. But I don't know anything about tailing someone. What if he sees us?"

"Well, to begin with, neither of you look remotely like a policeman, nor does Mr. Wesley know either of you. You would just be another of dozens of couples going about your business. You would not need to follow him closely. You would only need to keep a record of where he goes and generally, who he talks to. Have either of you ever used a camera with a telephoto lens?"

"Yeah, I have." Megan said, to my surprise. "I learned how to use one in art class."

"Splendid. So Mark can act as driver and you can take photographs from a safe distance."

"How long will we have to tail him?"

"Well, I can't say for sure. But if nothing of interest turns up after a day or two, I think we can safely assume he has not fallen for the bait."

"You mean we're going to have to stay up all night in our car, watching his house?" Megan asked.

"No. We will remain in contact by telephone. If by the end of the first day nothing has turned up, I will call him and suggest that it is important that I see him that evening. I will set the meeting for eight and then call him at ten with an excuse and my apologies. Hopefully that will keep him at home for the evening. The only thing I would suggest at that point is that you perhaps hire a rental car to use on the following day, in the unlikely event he has noticed your personal vehicle."

I looked over at Megan and shrugged my shoulders. She looked back with a conspiratorial grin.

"Let's do it. It'll be fun and at least we won't be sitting around another day not knowing what to do with ourselves."

"Very well then. If we are agreed I will contact you tomorrow and let you know as soon as I have set up my meeting with Mr. Wesley. Time is of the essence so I expect it will happen soon."

17

We were up late talking with Ham and I decided to take a room at the Marriott so we would be close by and wouldn't have to drive back up to Boca. I phoned Jennifer the following morning, after Megan had gone out for an early morning walk on the beach. I waited until I was sure the kids would be in school. She was relieved to hear from me but she pressed me pretty hard about what was going on. I explained the financial issues as best I could. She already knew that their home equity line of credit had been maxed out and there was not much left in their savings account. I could hear the fear and anger in her voice and she was trying very hard not to take it out on me. She seemed to sense I was hiding something and I was fighting the urge to just open up to her and tell her everything. I felt torn by my loyalty to Walt and my inclination to be completely honest with her. I didn't want to tell her anything that would threaten their marriage and a lot of what Walt had done needed to be dealt with privately between the two of them. Jen wanted to know what his mental state was and if he looked well or not. I told her he looked tired and stressed out but he seemed okay. I guess I justified not talking about the drugs because Walt had gone through detox and had quit using. I hoped it was true. Jen asked me to call her right away when I talked to him again, and I promised I would. When I hung up the phone it felt like I was the one who had gone off the rails.

We met Ham for lunch and he brought along a Nikon digital camera fitted with a telephoto lens. He handed it to Megan.

"A gift for you my dear, for your courage and your kind heart."

Megan looked shocked.

"This is for me to keep? Really? But you must use this all the time. In your work I mean. I can't take this."

"Actually I don't use it much at all. I have a new one which is a little better suited to my needs. It is fitted with a Macro lens for close-up, detail work. I have a telephoto lens as well so it serves both purposes. This one is still in very good shape though. I've had it for less than a year. It would please me to see you enjoy it."

"Thank you so much. I don't know what to say."

He spent some time showing Megan how to use the camera but she was a quick study and wanted to take it out on the patio right away to practice. Once again, she was like a kid at Christmas and I was glad she had something to take her mind off of things. After she left, Ham moved over and sat closer to me.

"You know, aside from my interest in the Great Omar, I have become quite attached to you and Megan. She has a delightful way about her and I must say I think what you are doing for her is quite admirable. I'm afraid this quest we are on, however, has taken a somewhat dangerous turn. I did not anticipate it would get to this point. The arrival of Mr. Alfarsi on the scene is a somewhat ominous sign and there has already been more than enough chaos surrounding the Omar to make me wary. No amount of money is worth putting Megan's life in danger, or yours."

I just nodded my head. I had already thought about it and came to the same conclusion. By now I was beginning to believe that getting the book was just a pipedream. It was sounding less and less likely by the day.

"I don't want to alarm Megan unnecessarily, so I will put it to you. If at any point you feel either of you may be in danger, I would implore you to walk away and get as far away from this as possible. I appreciate very much your assistance with this investigation, but I have other resources to bring to bear should that be necessary. I intend to pursue this search to its conclusion if that is at all possible. If I am able to secure the Great Omar, our bargain stands and I will make sure Megan receives what is due her. If anything should happen to me you may contact detective Benjamin. Keep your copy of our agreement in a safe place. I will provide you with my attorney's contact information."

"Do you think you're in danger, Ham?"

"Not yet. Not at the moment. However, once I show my hand to Mr. Wesley that could change. As I told you, I am, or rather I was a police detective. I am accustomed to dealing with dangerous and unsavory characters so I am not unduly concerned."

"It's not worth your life either, Ham."

"I appreciate you saying that. Truly. If the time comes that I feel I must also walk away I will do so. As I told you earlier, it is not about the money for me. If I miss my chance with the Omar I will be tremendously disappointed, but there are other lost treasures out there in the world to keep me busy. Now having said all of that, do you still wish to participate in our little surveillance ploy or would you prefer not to?"

"I don't think we would be in any real danger if we did this. Do you?"

"Actually no, I don't. Just keep your distance and don't under any circumstances take any action. Do not approach him no matter what the reason. If you think he has noticed you, drive away."

"We'll be careful, Ham. I'll ask Megan again if she really wants to do this but I already know the answer."

Ham had other work to do and he left as soon as Megan came back in. We spent the afternoon walking around Fort Lauderdale and taking pictures. I insisted on taking a few of Megan and she seemed to enjoy it for a change. She had finally come to trust me enough to allow

266

a few unguarded moments. We went down to the cruise ship terminal and Megan pretended we were about to sail away to some exotic island. I knew that I had become a witness to something rare in this world. Megan's life was opening like a flower right before my eyes. As I watched her emerge from her long isolation I began to see who she really was and who she could become if only she could let go of her past. I think it was at that moment that I realized I was in love with her.

I didn't say anything about my conversation with Ham and she didn't seem to want to talk about any of it. When I tried to bring it up, she quickly changed the subject.

"So I've been wanting to ask you what happened with your wife. It's okay if you don't want to talk about it."

"You mean how did she die?"

"Well that to. You said you were already separated when it happened?"

"Well, we weren't actually separated in the legal sense. The marriage counselor thought it would be a good idea if we spent some time apart. He thought it might make us realize what we missed about each other. Ann had a sister out in San Francisco. She went out there to spend some time with her. While she was there she met another guy. He was a Marine Biologist apparently. He took her Scuba diving. That was pretty much it."

"Were you hurt?"

"I was more sad than hurt. I guess I already knew it was over. I just didn't want to admit it."

"So how did it happen?"

"They were out at a bar. On the way home the car went off the road and into a ditch. Her boyfriend was drunk. Almost twice the legal limit they said. He survived. Ann was killed instantly."

"I'm really sorry. That must have been hard."

"Yeah. Until the accident I thought there still might be a chance. I thought maybe it was just a fling and she would get tired of it. The thing is, Ann was never a big drinker. She would never let me drive if I had more than one or two drinks. I'm sure she knew he was drunk. I sure she asked him to let her drive. I wanted to go out there and kill him."

"And this was a year ago?"

"Eleven months and some."

"So what have you been doing since?"

"Just working really. Our friends tried to cheer me up and get me out of the house, but they're all married couples. I felt like I didn't fit in."

"Did you try dating or anything?"

"Not in the beginning. Not for six months or so. A couple I know set up a double date with a woman friend. She was nice but I just wasn't ready to get into anything. I don't think I even know how to start a relationship any more. We were young when we got together."

"You're still young."

"It's not the years so much. When you're in your early twenties everyone is single and it's easy to meet people. You go and hang out and it just kind of happens. Once you get on with your life you have to plan everything. I just didn't feel like bothering with it."

"You just haven't met the right one yet?"

"I don't think I would know the right one from any other one."

"You'll know. She'll tell you."

Ham reached us in our room after dinner with news that he had arranged a meeting with Wesley at his house, at 10 AM the following morning. Megan was out on the balcony enjoying the mild breeze. I shouted out to her that we were on for tomorrow and she seemed excited about it. She was shooting pictures of the moonrise and refused to come back in.

"I hope you're leaving enough room in there for the pictures we'll have to take tomorrow."

"You don't need to worry about that. This thing has a huge memory card. Besides, I'm going to delete a lot of what I shot today. I was just getting used to the camera. There are a couple I'd like to keep though. Maybe we could print them out tomorrow if we have time."

"Sure. I imagine they have a printer for use by their guests. I want to keep a couple of you also."

She finally came back in and flopped down on the bed.

"Do you think this is really going to work?"

"I wouldn't get my hopes up, Megan. I think it's a long shot, but you never know. At least it will give us something to do."

"We should get some food and drinks and stuff for tomorrow. To have with us in the car, I mean. And I want to buy a disguise."

"What do you mean a disguise?"

"A pair of those Groucho Marx glasses with the fake nose and the hairy eyebrows."

I started laughing. "We're not supposed to be drawing attention to ourselves."

"We wouldn't be. Nobody could possibly know it was me. And you should get a blond wig and some fake boobs. No one would ever recognize us. I could dress up like a guy and you could wear a dress. It would be perfect."

She came over and sat next to me on the bed. I was still laughing at her.

"What? I'm serious, really."

"I can see that you are."

"Really. I want to see what you look like in a blond wig. I bet you would look hot."

Before I could respond she had climbed onto my lap and pushed me down onto the bed. She was in a playful mood and I was laughing too hard to be serious about it. We got into a wrestling match and we both ended up on the floor tangled in the bedspread.

18

Wesley's house was west of Miami in Hialeah. In the Roaring Twenties it had been a playground for the rich with its famous race track and pink flamingos. Now the city had a distinct Cuban flavor. The clerk at the convenience store where we waited spoke Spanish with most of the customers. Wesley lived out near the track on a quiet street lined with tall, Queen Palm trees. We were about a block away but had a good view of his house and driveway. He emerged about a half hour after Ham left the house. Megan was watching him through the camera.

"Does he look upset?"

"I have no idea what upset would look like. I never saw the guy before."

"Well I was hoping for something like him puking on the lawn."

"No such luck." She said, laughing.

Wesley was driving a vintage, black Mercedes Benz that issued a puff of gray smoke every time the gears were shifted. I kept a few cars between us as he headed downtown. We could almost keep track of him by following the diesel fumes. He stopped at a Starbucks and then spent some time in a Navarro pharmacy. Megan wanted to take pictures of everything but I managed to keep her focused for the most part. We spent a lot of time sitting in parking lots and waiting. It was beginning to look like a wasted exercise. We followed him into the business district past the Telemundo headquarters on 8th Avenue. It was a little tricky staying with him with the traffic lights. I didn't want to follow too closely and I went through a couple of red lights as I tried to keep him in sight. It was harder than I thought. Finally he pulled into a parking space near a Bank of America branch on 68th street. Megan started taking pictures in rapid fire, like a newspaper photographer. I couldn't find a parking space so I double parked and put on my flashers. Wesley opened his trunk and removed a brown, leather briefcase and then headed toward the bank. Cars were pulling up behind me and honking their horns. I was about to take a loop around the block when someone pulled out of a space ahead of us and I managed to park.

"I'm going to follow him." Megan said.

"You can't do that, Megan."

"Why? This is stupid. We don't have a clue about what he's about to do in there. He could be opening a savings account for all we know. At least if we could find out if he is going to a safe deposit box. He doesn't know me."

"Remember what Ham said?"

She opened her door. "I don't care."

I grabbed her by the arm. "Okay. But let me go then."

"Why not me?"

"Because people look at pretty young women. Nobody is going to take a second look at me. Now keep the doors locked and don't do anything to get yourself noticed. Try to keep that camera out of sight too. We don't need you getting mugged for it."

Wesley had already entered the bank and I jogged down the street and across the intersection. I slowed down when I got to the entrance and then I walked in and made my way to a counter where the forms were kept. Wesley was waiting outside one of the cubicles. He looked to be in his late forties with dark hair and a thin moustache that he kept neatly trimmed. He was well dressed, in slacks and a sport coat, but he had a seedy look about him. Like somebody you might see hanging around a betting parlor. He was staring off into space, oblivious to everything going on around him. His heel was bouncing up and down and he looked to me like he wanted to jump up and run away. I kept my head down and started writing on a deposit slip. Nobody seemed to be watching me but I took my time and then I tore up the slip and took a new one from the stack. After a minute or two, Wesley was waved into the cubicle and after a short conversation he reemerged with the bank officer who was holding a large ring of keys. My heart started to race. It appeared Ham's intuition had been right. The only thing I couldn't know was whether Wesley had the Omar in his briefcase and was about to place it in a box, or whether it was already at the bank and he was going to move it. Or maybe it had nothing to do with the Omar at all. I hurried out of the bank and jogged back to the car.

"Ham was right. He went for a safe deposit box."

Megan's eyes went wide and she was almost stuttering.

"You mean he really has the book with him? Holly crap. It's actually right there in that building. What should we do? We need to do something."

"I'm going to call Ham. Remember, we haven't actually seen the book. He could be putting anything in that box. Or taking anything out for that matter. Make sure your camera's ready. We need to get some shots of him coming out of the bank."

I punched in Ham's cell number but it rolled over to voice mail. Megan looked over at me.

"So what do you think? I think he had the book at his house and now he's putting it somewhere safer."

"I guess that's what I think, but if I had something like that with me I don't think I would leave it in my trunk while I went shopping for aspirin. There's no way to know. We'll just have to follow him and see where he goes next.

I tried Ham's cell a second time but got his voice mail again. I left a message asking him to call. Megan was as nervous as a squirrel and she kept checking the settings on the camera and focusing on the bank entrance. I was looking at the traffic in my rearview mirror. The building behind us was undergoing some construction and the area in front of it was roped off and partially blocked by a dumpster. A cement truck had pulled up to the building and it almost had me pinned in. I was trying to figure the best way to maneuver out of my spot when I heard Megan gasp. I looked over at her and she had a panicked look on her face.

"What's wrong?"

"She pointed at the bank. It's him. Jesus, what the hell is happening? Oh my god."

"Who? What are you talking about?"

She handed me the camera. "Look at that guy standing at the corner of the bank. The one smoking a cigarette."

I looked at him through the camera. He was wiry looking, with an angular face and olive colored skin. His hair and beard were black and close-cropped.

"That's him. That's the creepy guy who was following me in New York."

"Are you sure?" I said, looking back through the camera.

"I'm sure. I could never forget that face. What the hell is he doing here? How could he find me all the way down here? Oh my god. He must have been following us from the beginning."

I thought about it for a moment. It just didn't make any sense. I was sure we would have noticed him at some point. There was no way he could have followed us to Durham and waited in a car all night. Then suddenly, I understood. I reached over and put my hand on her arm.

"Calm down Megan. I don't think he's here for you at all. Remember that guy Ham was talking about? The one he saw talking to Wesley at the auction. He had an Arabic name. Some big time art dealer from New York. Alfarsi, I think. I bet this guy works for him. It all makes sense now. He was probably watching Annabel's house, hoping to find the book. That's why you started seeing him after you visited her. That's why he broke into your friend's apartment. He probably thought Annabel might have given the book to you. He's not looking for you. He's looking for the Great Omar. He's doing exactly what we're doing. Trying to get the book from Wesley."

I gave the camera back to her.

"Are you okay? I can drive us out of here if you want."

"No. I guess you're right. I just don't want to be anywhere near that creep."

She looked back through the camera in time to see Wesley emerge from the bank. He was carrying the briefcase and didn't look like he was in any hurry. We watched, fascinated as the man fell in behind him, and quickly closed the gap until he was right behind Wesley. Megan had the presence of mind to keep snapping pictures. I knew down deep that something bad was about to happen. When it did, it was so fast no one on the street seemed to notice. Wesley had just reached the other side of the intersection and was walking along the side of a building. The man pulled something out of his pocket and, struck Wesley at the base of his skull. Wesley fell to his knees and then flopped forward onto the sidewalk. The man took the briefcase without missing a step, and just continued walking down the street as if nothing had happened. He was moving quickly but not running. I realized, almost too late that he was going to walk right past out car. I put my hand on the back of Megan's head and pulled her over toward me as if we were about to kiss. Her whole body was trembling. The man stopped at the car immediately ahead of us and put the briefcase on the hood. He took a quick look back to make sure no one had seen him and then he turned in our direction. I watched him out of the corner of my eye. It seemed like he was looking right at us. I held Megan tightly in case she couldn't resist the urge to look at him.

"Keep still, Megan. Don't look at him."

He opened the briefcase and then yelled something I couldn't make out, staring up at the sky. He kicked the side of the car and then slammed the briefcase closed and continued down the street. As he passed the dumpster, he backed up a step and tossed the briefcase in. Then he turned and took another casual glance behind him. Wesley was still not moving. He crossed the street and disappeared down a side alley.

By then, people had noticed Wesley slumped against the building and a woman was leaning over him and trying to help. It was time for us to get out of there. I started the engine and was about to pull out of my spot when a thought came to me.

"Wait here a moment, Megan. Keep your head down."

I got out of the car and walked over to the dumpster. It was almost full with construction debris. I quickly pulled myself up and reached inside. I grabbed the briefcase by its side and pulled it toward me, trying to avoid touching the handle. I returned to the car, and threw the briefcase in the back seat. A cop was now stooped down tending to Wesley who had still not moved. As we were pulling away an ambulance arrived.

"Don't you think we should talk to the police about this?" Megan asked.

"Yeah. But I want to talk to Ham's friend, detective Benjamin. I want him to be able to examine this briefcase before it gets returned to Wesley or buried in some evidence locker."

19

Ham finally called on our way back to the hotel. I told him what had happened and he was alarmed. Especially when I told him about Megan's run-in with the attacker in New York City. His meeting with Wesley had not gone well and he had already decided it was time to lay out his tale of the Great Omar for detective Benjamin. He was on his way to meet him, and suggested we come along. He gave me the address and I entered it into my GPS. Ham was waiting for us when we arrived at the police station.

Benjamin's office was piled high with file boxes and one entire wall was covered with photographs of what were presumably, stolen art objects. He apologized for the cramped quarters. He was tall with graying hair and wire-rimmed glasses. He was wearing a tweed sport coat with patches at the elbow. There was a studious look about him. I never would have guessed he had anything to do with police work.

"Sorry for the cramped quarters. This is not what you would call a high-profile task force." He said, pointing to the stacks of folders. "Let me see if one of the interrogation rooms is available."

He stopped at a coffee urn in the hallway and filled his cup, inviting us to help ourselves. We all took seats around a bare metal table. There was nothing else in the room. Because of what had just happened to Wesley, Ham thought it would be prudent to start with that. I was as straightforward as possible. I didn't get into detail as to why we were watching Wesley but I told him what we had witnessed and Megan was able to show him some excellent pictures of the attacker, including one of him standing over Wesley as he slumped to the pavement. Benjamin called a uniformed officer in and he took the camera out to print some stills. I showed him the briefcase and explained that I had fished it out of a dumpster.

"You realize you should have given this to the officers at the scene."

"Well, I knew we had to hand it over to the police. That's why I'm giving it to you."

"Would you like to explain why you were tailing Mr. Wesley?"

"I think I'd like to leave that to Ham if you don't mind. I think after you hear his story you'll understand why. I haven't opened the briefcase, by the way, and I didn't touch the handle."

He nodded and turned to Ham.

"So what do you have to tell me?"

Ham launched into an abbreviated history of the Great Omar. He was careful to explain how Megan had become involved and he showed Benjamin the letter from Annabel Weiss giving the Great Omar to Megan. The detective seemed fascinated and at several points he asked Ham to provide more detail. He was particularly interested in Ham's detective work and how he had reached his conclusions. It took nearly a half hour to fill in the background and bring the story up to the auction where he had seen Wesley negotiating with the Iranian art dealer. They were talking about Wesley's background when the officer returned with Megan's camera and a number of eight by ten photographs of Wesley's attacker. He showed them to Benjamin and then asked to speak to him privately. They stepped out of the room.

"Do you think they'll get this guy?" Megan asked.

"I have no doubt they will and when they do it won't take long to get him convicted, thanks to you. I have to commend the both of you for your work today. I could not have done it better myself. I'm sorry you had to be a witness to that violence, Megan. I won't ask you to do anything like that again. I think what you saw today is a clear indication of what Alfarsi is willing to do to get his hands on the Great Omar."

"How can we be sure he's behind all this? Couldn't this guy be acting on his own?"

"I doubt that very much. I'm convinced he is working for someone. If not Alfarsi, then someone else with connections in the art world."

Benjamin returned after about ten minutes and pulled a full face shot of the attacker out of the pile of photographs.

"Well it wasn't difficult finding this guy. Did he see either of you today?"

"Not really. At least I'm sure he didn't get a clear look at our faces. We were pretty careful."

"But you're sure this is the man who confronted you in New York."

"Yeah. I'm sure. It was right after Annabel, I mean Ms. Weiss, told me about the book."

"And he didn't recognize you today?"

"I don't think so. I'm sure he would have reacted."

"I hope that's the case. This is someone with a long history of violence, and you would not want to make any direct contact with him. It turns out there is a very large jacket on this individual. His given name is Khalil Badra. In New York City he is know as the Algerian, although his country of birth is actually Tunisia. His street name is Sabat, which means the Spider. He is somewhat of a thug for hire among other things. He specializes in second story jobs. Hence the nickname."

"What kind of jobs?" Megan asked

"I'm sorry. Burglaries that are done by scaling a building and making entry through un-alarmed windows on the upper floors. He also has a very long list of convictions for petty crimes including shoplifting and simple assaults. He is known to prey on prostitutes, beating and robbing them. He has been questioned several times in murders of prostitutes and homeless individuals, but there was never enough evidence to indict him for any of those crimes."

Megan shivered and looked down at the floor.

"He has one felony assault conviction for the armed robbery of a stock broker in Penn Station. He did six years on Rikers Island for that one. The Homeland Security people questioned him after nine-eleven but he was not held. He does not appear to have ties with any Islamic groups, radical or otherwise and he is not known to attend a mosque. We were not aware of his presence here in South Florida until now. We will shortly have his picture distributed to every law enforcement officer in the area. We should be able to apprehend him in short order. If you come into contact with this individual again, please call the police immediately. I would also caution you to leave the police work to us in the future. For your own good."

"Do you find any connection in your files between this individual and Mr. Alfarsi?" Ham asked.

"Not so far, but I think you are probably correct in your assumption. It would be unlikely for someone like Badra to stray so far from his home turf on his own. He is likely down here because he's working for someone. After the events of today and what you have told me about Mr. Wesley, I think it's a reasonable suspicion that Badra and Alfarsi are connected. In any case, we'll be keeping an eye on Mr. Alfarsi. His name has come up several times in connection with major art thefts, as you know. It would not be a surprise to find out he's up to no good."

"What about the briefcase." I asked.

"Well, we are on somewhat shaky ground on that issue. If you had picked it up from the street near the incident it would no doubt be regarded as obviously Mr. Wesley's personal property and we could not open it without a court order. Since you found it in a public dumpster and there is no identification on the outside of the case, I believe the courts would rule it would be reasonable for the police to open the case to try to identify the owner. I will have the handle dusted for prints first, and then we'll take a look inside. It's pretty dirty from being in the dumpster but we'll see what we can find. I would also ask if you would voluntarily provide us with elimination prints as well, Mr. Macmillan, since you handled the case. I have to caution you that nothing we find inside would likely stand up as evidence, nor could we take any kind of action based solely on what we may find there. That being said, I would appreciate you assistance, Ham, in taking a look at anything we find inside as a consultant to the Miami Beach police department. Unfortunately, it isn't a paid position."

We took a break then. They took my fingerprints and dusted the briefcase as well. They wanted to take Megan's prints also but she refused, insisting that she had not touched the case. Everyone was waiting for me when I returned to the interrogation room, still trying to clean the ink off of my fingers with a paper towel. The officer returned in a moment and put the briefcase on the table.

"You and Megan may observe, Mr. Macmillan, but please do not touch anything."

I already knew from Badra's reaction when he opened the case that we would not find the Omar inside. Still my heart was racing when Benjamin open it there in front of us. There was nothing at all in the main compartment. There were several file slots inside the top of the case and they held a number of documents. Ham and Benjamin read through them one by one. Nothing seemed to be related to Alfarsi except for a business card with his name on it and a New York address. Ham was clearly disappointed. Megan had been looking over Ham's shoulder when suddenly she said. "Hey, what's that?"

Everyone looked at her.

"What's what?" I asked

She pointed.

"There, in the case down in the corner."

Benjamin looked where Megan was pointing and then he reached in and pinched something between his fingertips. He put it down on one of the documents. It looked like a glass bead. We all stared at it in silence.

"Do you have a magnifying glass, by any chance, detective?"

Benjamin left the office and returned in a moment with a jeweler's loupe. He gave it to Ham.

Ham examined the small object under the loupe, moving it around with the tip of his pen.

"Well, it appears to be a genuine gemstone. There are no air bubbles which would indicate a piece of glass, and there are some inclusions which would be expected. The color is good but not up to say the Burmese variety. If I'm not mistaken, what we have here is a small natural ruby."

"I knew it! Megan shouted. That's got to be from the book doesn't it? That's part of the Great Omar."

We were all a little stunned, just staring at the small gem in silence.

The detective left the room and returned with a plastic evidence bag. He wrote some information on the outside of the bag and then dropped the small jewel in and sealed it.

"Well if the stone did indeed come from the Great Omar,' Ham said, there is a high probability we now know its location. It would appear the book is currently in Mr. Wesley's safe deposit box."

There was a long silence then as we each considered the implications of what Ham had just said.

"Do we know Mr. Wesley's condition?" Ham asked. "Was he admitted into the hospital?"

"No, but I can find out." He left the room again.

"It would appear this is good news for us." Ham said. "I don't believe there was much trust between Wesley and Alfarsi to begin with. After this incident I would think it very unlikely Wesley would want to have any further dealings with him. He is also, no doubt, extremely frightened. I think it may be time to pay Mr. Wesley another visit. Are you still willing to offer a finders fee for the return of the book, Megan?"

"Sure. Won't he be arrested though, for having it in the first place?"

"Perhaps not. There are often considerations made in exchange for the return of a high value item such as the Omar. Remember, there has been no criminal complaint. As you have seen, detective Benjamin had no idea the book was in play prior to our conversation today. I believe something could be worked out."

Megan started to say something when Benjamin came back in.

"Mr. Wesley is currently at Palmetto General Hospital in Hialeah. He is in guarded condition and has not regained consciousness. They believe he will recover but there is no way to know whether he has sustained any long term damage. I advised the Hialeah PD that we have

Mr. Wesley's briefcase and they'll send someone over to pick it up. I also faxed over the photographs and a description of Khalil Badra. If he is still in the area they will likely find him soon."

"Assuming Mr. Wesley recovers and is able to talk. I would like to pay him a visit and see if he has changed his mind about giving up the book." Ham said.

Benjamin nodded his head. "I'll need to come along. Otherwise they may not let you talk to him. I want to talk to him anyway. Maybe he can tell us how Badra knew to find him at the bank. It could be he was just tailing Wesley as you two were. But there's also the possibility Wesley was working on some deal with Alfarsi. It seems like Badra was expecting to find the book after Wesley left the bank. I don't think we've seen to the bottom of this thing yet."

20

The next morning, Megan and I checked out of the Marriott and drove back to Boca Raton. Ham said he would feel better if Megan were someplace safe while he and detective Benjamin continued their investigation. There was really nothing we could do anyway. Megan busied herself taking pictures of everything she found interesting. Again it seemed like she had lost interest in the book. She still didn't want to talk about it, or about anything else for that matter. I didn't pressure her. It was as if the closer she got to actually having the Omar, the more she was in denial about it. I think she didn't want to have to face the changes it was going to bring to her life. The idea of suddenly having all of that money scared her. Not so much the wealth itself, but everything that would come with it. She knew, I think, that no matter how hard she fought to hold on, it was going to change the order of things. I think she truly believed there was no way for her to be Megan, except in that rare and fascinating world she had constructed in her mind. The world she had been drawing for me since I met her at that rest stop on the turnpike all those days ago. To separate her from that was to cast her adrift in a very lonely and frightening place.

"Maybe you could start a career in photography." I said after the silence began to become uncomfortable.

"Maybe, but there are a zillion people doing that. I'm more interested in using it to get ideas for drawings and paintings. This telephoto lens is really cool. You can get shots of things in the distance but there's not much depth of field. The thing you focus on is sharp but the image looks flat. Almost two dimensional. Anything behind it or in front of it is kind of blurry. You can get some cool effects. When I get time I want to set up an easel and play around with it a little bit you know, do some paintings of things from a different perspective."

"That sounds interesting. Maybe we could get you some paint and brushes and you could start one while were waiting."

"No, I'm not ready for that yet. I just want to experiment with the camera for a while."

"Looks like you know what you're doing. I'm impressed."

"I'm really not very good with it. I just learned a little in art class, like I said. Enough to have some fun with it anyway."

She spent another five minutes or so taking pictures and then she turned the camera off and put it beside her on the seat. She turned to me.

"I'm sorry. I didn't mean to be ignoring you. I just never had a camera of my own like this before. It was really nice of Ham to give it to me. I really like him. I mean, even if he hadn't given it to me."

"He likes you too. Anyway, I'm glad you're enjoying yourself."

"What about you. Are you enjoying yourself?"

"Yeah, I really am. I haven't been bored once since I met you."

"I'm sorry for taking up all your time. I'll bet you haven't thought once about what you're going to do after this is all over with."

"You're right, but I'm not in any rush. I don't think that's what I need to be doing right now anyway. I want to take my time with it."

"You mean you're putting it off."

"Exactly." I said, smiling.

"Yeah, me too. But that's good anyway. I'm not done with you're attitude adjustment yet." She said, laughing.

"Is that what you're doing with me?"

"Well. I'm not actually doing anything. It's like catching a cold. If you hang out with me long enough you're going get infected. Pretty soon you're going to start to sneeze. Who knows, you might end up fishing people out of fountains."

I started to respond when my phone rang. It was Walt and he was in a dead panic. I listened to him for a moment and then muted the phone.

"It's Walt. He wants to meet me as soon as I can manage. He's over in Coral Springs. It's not far from here. Would you mind if I dropped you off at the hotel while I talk to him."

"If it's close, why don't I just come with you?"

"I don't know if he would feel free to talk with you there."

"Well, if it's about his rehab I might be able to help. If he doesn't want me there I can wait in the car. I don't mind."

"Are you sure?"

"Positive."

I got back on with Walt and asked where we could meet. He wanted someplace quiet and suggested the library over on University Drive.

"Are you going to talk to him about the heroin?"

"I don't know what he wants to talk about."

"Can I give you some advice?"

"Sure."

"Well if you do, try not to judge him. He doesn't need that right now. You need to build him up. Tell him how strong he is for getting control of it. It's important to make him feel good about getting clean. He's going to be really fragile for a while and really down on himself. You don't want to make it worse."

"Does that help?"

"I think so. I've been around people in rehab. A lot of them go through it over and over. They just can't stay clean. Your friend has a good chance of making it because he has a life to go back to and people that love him. It's harder for people out on the street. A lot of them hate themselves to begin with and their world really sucks. They don't have any good reason to try. They just want to go to sleep and make it all go away."

It took us a half hour to drive to Coral Springs and find the library. I brought Megan in with me to meet Walt. He looked a little wary, but Megan excused herself and went to look for some photography books. We found a table in the back. I could see the panic on his face. He didn't look much better than the last time I saw him.

"Charley's dead."

I just stared at him for a moment, as my mind raced through all the implications of what he had just told me.

"You mean somebody killed him?"

"No, they threatened him, but they didn't hurt him at all. He had a heart attack at work. He just slumped over on his desk and that was it. How could this be happening to me, Mark? It's like all of a sudden I have some big fucking bull's eye on my back."

"It's not all about you, Walt. Didn't Charley have a family?"

"Yeah. I'm sorry, I don't mean to sound like an asshole, it's just that it's all on me now. Everything. The whole debt."

"Have they talked to you about it?"

"No, but they came to the house. Jesus, they scared Jen half to death. They told her if I didn't meet them by the end of this week there would be consequences."

"What are you going to do?"

"I don't know. I'm on my way back up to North Carolina for Charley's funeral. It's time for me to sit down with Jen and come clean about everything for starters. I don't know if she's going to be able to take it. I'm afraid she's going to leave me."

"She's a strong woman, Walt, and I know she loves you. I'm sure you can make this right.

It's going to take some time. You need to tell her everything. All of it. If you hold back and she finds out later, she'll never be able to trust you again. Does she know you're on your way back?"

"Yeah. I talked to her last night. I really fucked up, Mark. I can't even see how I'm going to get through this."

"How much do you owe?"

"A hundred thousand."

"Jesus. Do they want it all at once?"

"No, but they're going to charge me 15 percent interest until it's paid off. They want twenty thousand by the end of the week. I'm going to meet with them when I get up there and try to work out some terms. I'm going to make sure they understand they can't go near Jennifer again."

"Be careful Walt. They don't sound like the kind of people you can intimidate."

"I don't give a damn. If they go near her again, I'm going to kill them."

"Use your head. Don't make it worse than it already is."

"Don't worry. I can handle it. I have a gun if it comes to that."

I just looked at him for a moment. An overwhelming feeling of sadness came over me. I had always thought he was the stronger of the two of us. He always had this unshakable confidence in himself, and until now he had made a success out of everything he tried. Now it seemed he had come completely undone. Part of me wanted to smack some sense into him but it was too late for that. For the first time, I found myself wondering myself whether he was going to make it, but I had to help him if I could. I took out my checkbook.

"Okay, Walt. I'll write you a check for the twenty grand."

"Jesus, thanks Mark. I hate to put you through this. I really do. I just don't have anyone else to turn to."

"Do you have any way to get the rest of the money? You told me Charlie was trying to sell your program."

"Yeah and he got some people interested. I'm going to talk to them after the funeral. You'll get this money back, Mark. I swear it."

"It can wait. You need to get this straightened out first. What about the drugs? Are you still clean?"

"Yeah. So far I'm holding it together, but I want to use all the time. It's all of this crap that's happening. I'm so wired I'm afraid I might have a stroke or something. They say it gets easier, I don't know. I've never been through something like this before. It's taking all my strength and it's hard for me to concentrate."

"Just think about Jen and the kids. You have a lot of reasons to get this all behind you."

"I know. That's what's keeping me going. If it wasn't for them I don't think I'd make it."

"Don't talk like that. You're stronger than that. You screwed up but you'll get through this. Don't they have meetings for people who are recovering from Heroin? Like AA meetings. Where you can get support?"

"Yeah. I was going to them down in Key Largo. I'll find a group up in Durham once I get this straightened out. I hated going to them but they do help. They don't let you lie to yourself about it."

"Listen, Mark. If anything happens to me I want you to make sure Jen and the kids are okay. Can you promise me that?"

"Of course, but it's not going to come to that. You can do this."

"I don't have much left to give them but I still have a life insurance policy. It's a half a million. It should be enough for her to keep the house and help get the kids through college. I don't want the kids to think I was some kind of bad person. I want' them to know I love them."

"They don't need the money as much as they need you. Call me when you get up there and let me know how it's going, will you."

"Yeah. I will."

"Do you want the thumb drive back?"

"No. I'd like you to hold onto that a little longer if you don't mind. It this all goes well, I won't need it."

"Why don't you just give it to these people you owe the money to. Just get it over with."

"I'm not ready to give it up yet. Besides, it's not as simple as that. They wouldn't know how to use it. I would have to stay involved with them and that's the last thing I want. I still think I can find a buyer. I'll only do that if I don't have any other choice."

"It sounds like you might be at that point now."

"Not yet. I still think I can sell this thing."

On the way back to the condo, Megan asked me about the conversation. I filled her in the best I could. When I finished she turned and looked at me.

"I think he's still using."

"Why. What makes you think so?"

"I don't know for sure. But he looks like it to me. I've seen it before."

"Jesus. I hope you're wrong."

"So do I."

21

Ham and detective Benjamin visited Wesley in his hospital room the following morning. He had regained consciousness during the night and they performed a CAT scan. There didn't seem to be any permanent damage. Ham said Wesley initially denied everything, but when they showed him the photographs of Badra attacking him and detailed his history of violent crimes, he finally relented. Ham didn't even have to offer the finders fee. All Wesley wanted in the end was Benjamin's word that he would not be prosecuted for taking the book. He claimed Alvarez had given it to him before he died but when he was pressed for proof, he crumbled. What he refused to do was to implicate Alfarsi in any way or to admit he had been working on a deal with him. He wanted to know if the police had any leads on Badra and whether they thought he was still in the area. He was clearly afraid for his safety.

Wesley was discharged early in the afternoon and he agreed to accompany Benjamin to the bank to retrieve the Great Omar. The detective asked Ham to wait for him back at the police station so he could authenticate the book. Ham called and asked us to drive down and meet him there. He was so excited you could almost hear the grin in his voice. We were all sitting in the interrogation room when Benjamin came in carrying a cardboard box. He opened it and placed the book, which was wrapped in tissue paper, in front of us on the table. Ham carefully opened the wrapping and we all went silent. It glowed in the harsh light like a brick of solid gold. The gems looked like a thousand small fires burning from deep within the binding. The detailed craftsmanship on the cover was stunning. We just sat there for a moment, at a loss for words.

"After all these years, and all those people who died. I can't believe this thing is here on the table in front of us. This book was actually on the Titanic and it survived. I'm afraid to even touch it." Megan said.

"Let's allow Ham to perform his evaluation first." Benjamin said.

Ham reached into his briefcase and removed a pair of white cotton gloves. He carefully slid the book over in front of him. You could see the excitement on his face. It was almost as if he were holding some sacred relic from the Vatican. First he looked over every inch of the cover with a large magnifying glass. He asked Benjamin if he could bring in the gem they had found when they examined Wesley's briefcase. Benjamin returned and gave the evidence bag to Ham. He removed a pair of tweezers from his case and carefully picked up the stone. He pressed it onto the cover of the book.

"This appears to be a perfect fit. I believe I can say with confidence that the stone was dislodged from this very binding."

Next he slid his index finger under the edge of the cover and gently lifted it until it was vertical. He examined the inside of the binding with his magnifier as he gently moved the cover and then some of the interior pages back and forth.

"There has been some deterioration as is to be expected but I don't see any signs of mold. This book was bound in a method called Japanese Stab Sewing. There has been some cutting into the leaf but the threads appear to be largely intact. We should not open the front or rear covers at more than ninety degrees to avoid splitting the spine. All in all, the book has been preserved quite well, for having gone down with the Titanic." He said, grinning. "Ironically, all of those years hidden inside that bible seem to have slowed the natural deterioration somewhat. It's in remarkably good condition."

He removed the loose stone and carefully turned the book over to reveal the rear cover with its gold inlay of a lute.

"Now let me show you all something not generally known about this binding."

He opened the rear cover.

"Do you see this border around the inside rear cover? That is what's known as the back doublure. Take a close look at it Megan."

Megan leaned over and in a few seconds she gasped.

"Oh my god. There's a scull in the picture with flowers growing out of its eye sockets."

"Not just any flower, my dear. Those are Poppies from which, as you no doubt know, both opium and heroin are derived. Known around the globe as the flower of death."

Megan shivered. "Oh my god, that's too creepy. No wonder the thing is cursed. Now I know I don't want to touch at it."

We spent nearly an hour going carefully through the book and looking at the beautiful illustrations. Only Ham actually handled the book to insure we didn't do any accidental damage. Ham removed his camera from its case and took detailcd photographs of the front and rear covers both inside and out and of the spine of the book. He also took pictures of all the internal details and illustrations. When he had finished we all sat in silence for a moment. Finally, Ham spoke to Benjamin.

"So what needs to happen now, so that Megan can take possession of this treasure?"

"Well, no one is contesting ownership nor, in spite of our suspicions, is there any concrete evidence that the book was ever part of the Alvarez collection. If it were, he would have had it illegally in any case. Mr. Wesley's claim of ownership can not be supported by any evidence, or he would have offered to produce it. You said you can get copies of the original ownership documents from Ms. Weiss' attorney. Once the documentation has been reviewed and authenticated, I see no reason why we shouldn't turn the book over to you Megan."

"Where will you keep it in the mean time?" Ham asked.

"We have a safe here in the building. Because of our taskforce we often have to securely store valuable objects of art until they can be returned to their owners. It's more to prevent damage in handling than anything else. There have been a few cases in the past of valuable items disappearing from the evidence locker but not on my watch. The book will be safe here."

"Very well." Ham said. "Unless you have any objections, Megan, I will contact Annabel's attorney and have the documents sent down to us by courier. It shouldn't take more than a couple of days. Also I will get in touch with my prospect and tell him we have the book. He will, of course want to see it for himself before we start negotiations."

Megan looked at me. "What am I going to do with it in the meantime? We can't just leave it hanging around the condo."

"We can put it into your safe deposit box. Until it's time to show it to a buyer."

"It'll never fit in there."

"So we'll rent a bigger one."

On the drive back, Megan was quiet. She still had a stunned expression on her face and I could almost see her mind racing. She looked over at me.

"I never really thought it was going to happen. Did you?"

"Probably not."

"It's funny you know. Everybody thinks it's so beautiful and it is, but I can't get past all the people who've died because of it. When I first saw it back at the police station it felt like I was seeing something evil. But it's just a thing after all. How can a thing be evil? How can it kill people?"

"Things don't kill people, Megan. Greed kills people."

"I guess, but there are other cursed things in the world. Isn't the Hope Diamond supposed to be cursed? I read once that one of the people who owned it was ripped apart by a pack of wild dogs and that some French noble who had it was beaten to death by a mob. I think Marie Antoinette owned it too, and look what happened to her. And then there's King Tut's tomb. I don't know."

"Maybe it has to do with your theory about fear. About fear causing bad things to happen."

"I don't know. I don't think Marie Antoinette was afraid to wear the Hope Diamond. And I don't think the guy who opened King Tut's tomb was afraid of it either. Some people believe there are blessed objects too. Like Relics and stuff. Things that can heal you or bring you good luck. I think it's two sides of the same coin. A friend of mine has a computer and sometimes we play games on it. One of them is like a treasure hunt. You go around trying to find valuable things, but some of them are booby trapped and when you open them they blow up and kill you. Maybe that's what the real world is like too. All I know is I want to sell it as fast as I can and I don't want it near me while I'm waiting. The more I think about that murderer Basra being right there in my face, the more I want to get away from it. Benjamin said he was suspected of killing homeless people in the city. I can't stop thinking I might have known somebody he killed."

22

The following morning we went to Megan's bank and rented a larger safe deposit box. I also gave her some money so she could open a checking account. It was the first time in her life she had her own ATM card and she insisted on withdrawing some cash. When the money came out she looked at me and laughed.

"Curiouser and curiouser. So this is how it feels to fall down the rabbit hole. Do you see a bottle anywhere that says drink me?"

"We'll find that tonight."

"Well, we'd better get home now before the Jabberwocky finds us."

That evening I kept my promise and rented a limo. We drove up to Palm Beach and had dinner at the Breakers to celebrate. Megan couldn't stop giggling. When she stepped out of the limo she was vamping like a movie star. She leaned over and whispered in my ear.

"Keep track of the time. At midnight this thing is going to turn into a pumpkin."

I let Megan choose the restaurant. There were eight of them on the property and she chose The Seafood Bar because it felt like being on a ship. I talked her into ordering the lobster tails and she laughed when they gave her a bib to wear. When they brought them out she wrinkled her nose.

"I feel like I'm eating a big bug."

We had champagne with dinner and Megan got a little tipsy. She was laughing and making fun of herself and of me. When we had finished dinner she insisted on taking her glass over to the aquarium bar so she could watch the fish while she got drunk. It seemed like the ocean was washing right up to our window. We stayed until she finished her champagne and then had the driver take us over to West Palm Beach for some nightlife. We rode around for a while, not sure where to go. Finally, Megan insisted we stop at a place she saw called the Blue Martini, just so she could drink something blue. We sat at the bar. She had this huge martini glass in front of her and she looked like a kid in an ice cream parlor.

She had finished about half of it when she looked down at the floor.

"I think that definitely made me larger." She said, laughing. "My feet seem much farther away then they used to."

"Well I think you'd better slow down there, Alice. The night is still young."

"Yeah and we haven't met the hookah smoking caterpillar yet."

"Just follow your nose; I'm sure he's around her someplace."

I asked the bartender where we could find some live music and he said there was a good band playing at Roxy's. Our driver knew where it was and when we got there I asked him to pull up by the front door. There was a long line of people waiting to get in and they were gawking at Megan, trying to figure out who she was. I took her by the arm and walked right up to the front of the line. I gave the bouncer a fifty dollar bill and he let us in with a flourish. Megan's grin was now permanently etched on her face. She had finally mastered the art of high heels and I think as the night went on she really was feeling more comfortable with herself. We watched for a while until Megan dragged me by the arm out onto the dance floor. She danced like a crazy woman and part of the time I just stood there watching her and laughing like I hadn't since forever. Everyone else was looking at her too, including a lot of guys who probably couldn't figure out what she was doing with an old dude like me. Megan was oblivious to it all. She had completely let go and the joy was radiating from her like a star. I don't think it had much to do with the money. It was more that at least for those few hours, she no longer felt like a misfit toy. For maybe the first time in her life, she was on the inside and didn't feel the need to feel guilty about it. I think she was starting to believe it was possible for her to have a different life. At one point they actually played something slow and she danced with her arms around my neck and her head buried against my chest. She felt as light as a feather in my arms. After a couple of hours we were both exhausted and we agreed to call it a night.

When we left I told the driver to take his time. I closed the partition so we could have some privacy. Megan stood with her head poking out of the sun roof and she insisted I join her. There was a thunder storm out at sea and we watched in awe as the lightning flashed across the dark sky, and the clouds on the horizon erupted in wild electric colors. The thunder rumbled in across the dark waters, vibrating in our chests. We could smell the ozone in the air. I looked at her with her hair blowing in the wind and a look of utter happiness on her face and I had to kiss her. Other drivers were waving and honking their horns at us as they passed. After a while the rain began to come down and we closed the sun roof. Megan threw her arms around me and pulled me down onto the seat. We made love with a passion I hadn't felt since I was first married. Megan was straddling me with the top of her dress pulled down and her small, perfect breasts rising in time with her breathing. Looking at me through half closed eyes as we moved together to the rhythm of the rain that was now pouring down in waves, and the tires singing on the wet pavement. The headlights of passing cars reflected through the window in rivulets of liquid light, running down her soft white skin. Like tears washing away the pain of a life lived too near the shadows, and too far from her dreams.

"I'll never forget this night." She said. "I'll never forget what you've done for me."

Later, I asked the driver to take us down to South Beach. We cruised the Art Deco streets, splashing through puddles smeared with neon light. Watching couples running through the rain and laughing. And holding onto each other in silence, in that warm, still place beyond words.

Megan fell asleep in my arms and I watched her drift away into her dreams. I could have held her there forever. I whispered in her ear.

"Welcome to your new life, Megan. I hope you're always as happy as you are tonight."

We both woke the next morning with hangovers and we spent half the day in bed. Megan was almost as funny with a hangover as she was drunk. She was walking around the condo like she was ninety years old, and warning me she was going to puke at any moment. We managed to get up in time for a late lunch. I knew a small café that served an all-day breakfast and we ordered some eggs and coffee.

"Has it settled in yet, Megan?"

"It's starting to."

"Have you thought about where you're going to live?"

"I'm thinking I'll go back to the city, at least for a while. I'll rent an apartment or something. I haven't gotten much further than that."

"Well, that's a start anyway. You'll have plenty of time to figure it all out."

"What about you?"

"No clue."

"What about us? Is there an us?"

I hesitated for a moment. I had been thinking about it for a while without coming up with a good answer. I just couldn't see how it would work. I loved being around her and I didn't want that to change, but I was convinced the age difference would become a problem sooner or later. I didn't want to jump into anything until we had things sorted out a little.

"You know I love you, Megan. How could you not know it?"

"That's not what I asked you. I love you too. I just need to know if you're still going to be around when this is all settled or are you going to just disappear out of my life."

"That's not going to happen. I can't imagine a world that doesn't have you in it. It's just that I'm a lot older than you. I think you need someone who's young like you are."

"I'm not young, I told you that. You can't live like I've been living and still be young. I've been around lots of young people. Guys my age. It's like I can see right through them. They seem like kids to me. I couldn't imagine having a serious relationship with any of them."

"I get that. I just think you need to settle into your new life a little bit before you decide what you want. It's all going to be brand new to you. Let's just give it some time."

"I don't know what a relationship is all about anyway. I don't ever want to be married. I don't really want kids; at least that's how I feel right now. I don't want anybody to own me. To tell me what I can do and who I can hang out with. What's that all about anyway? I don't get it."

"Most people want to have someone close. Somebody to share things with and to care for. Somebody to turn to when life gets tough. Not everybody has as much strength as you do, Megan."

"I get lonely too. I just don't want to give up my freedom just to have somebody there to hold my hand when I get scared."

23

Ham drove up and met us for lunch the following day. Again, he got right down to the business at hand without his usual polite banter. He seemed uneasy.

"I've been in contact with Ms. Weiss' attorney. We should have the documents by Friday morning. He also asked when you could be back in New York City for the reading of Annabel's will."

"Does that have to happen before I can get the book?"

"No, no. It's quite a separate matter than the ownership documents."

"Why do I need to go back up there then?"

It would seem you have been mentioned in Annabel's Will."

"What do you mean mentioned?"

"She has apparently left you some other items in addition to the Great Omar."

"What items?"

"I don't know, Megan. You'll find out when the Will is read."

"I hope she left me a couple of the things from her apartment. I'd love to have something around to remind me of her. I feel so guilty for not going to her funeral. I hope somebody was there for her."

"I was told by her lawyer that Annabel was quite active in her Synagogue and that her service was well attended. If that makes you feel any better. Under the circumstances, it would not have been possible for you to attend. Ms. Weiss, of all people, would have understood that."

"When I get back up to the city I want to put some flowers on her grave. Do you know where she's buried?"

"I'm sure her attorney will tell you when you meet him."

"Have you talked to the person who made you that offer on the book?" I asked.

"Not yet. He is currently out of the country and may not be back for another week or so. How long do you intend to stay here in Boca Raton?"

"We haven't made any plans yet. A while longer anyway."

"Very well. I'll let you know when I have some more definite information on the buyer. I'm afraid I have other business I must attend to, so I will have to ask you to excuse me. I'm sorry for the short visit. Perhaps we can all have dinner together sometime in the next day or two. Before I go, however, there is one additional matter I need to mention. I don't want you to be alarmed, but Mr. Wesley has been found dead in his home."

Megan gasped.

"How did he die?"

"Apparently he was stabbed during a burglary of his house. The place was ransacked."

"Oh my god." Megan said. "That asshole Badra killed him. I know it was him. He's still trying to find the book."

"That is one possibility, Megan, but you shouldn't leap to that conclusion. Detective

326

Benjamin told me there had been several muggings and break-ins in Wesley's neighborhood. It's the drugs, you know. It appears to be out of control down here. The police are investigating and they will, of course, dust for fingerprints. Badra's prints are in the system, so we'll see."

"Why would they want to kill him now anyway?" I asked.

"If he was killed over the book, it might indicate that they don't know we have it at the police station. Perhaps they think it was never removed from Wesley's residence. Or maybe they just wanted him silenced."

"It's because they're evil and they don't care who they kill. I can't wait to get rid of that thing. I don't even want to think about it anymore."

"Yes." Ham said. "Now that we have found it and had a chance to examine it, I will be somewhat relieved to move on as well."

The documents from Annabel's lawyer arrived on Friday as promised. We went over to the police station and brought the original of

Annabel's letter to Megan as further proof of ownership. Detective Benjamin examined everything and made photocopies. He had Megan sign some papers.

"As far as I'm concerned, there is no question the book belongs to Megan. I am going to release it to you this morning. I would ask you to be very cautious from this point on. If Alfarsi has interest in the book as we suspect, he will still be looking for it. Maybe he only wants to make an offer on it, however, recent events suggest otherwise. Mr. Wesley was beaten very badly before he was killed. It does appear someone was trying to get information out of him. Badra is still at large and although we don't have evidence of a connection at this time, that's our best guess."

"We're going to take it to the bank right now and put it in the safe."

"I think that would be a good idea. Would you like me to drive you, just in case?"

"No, but thank you for offering. I think we'll be fine."

"Please keep alert for anyone you see around you more than once or twice. Anyone who is taking more interest in you than they should.

There could be others involved. It's not clear if Badra knows you're down here, Megan, but I think there is a good possibility he does by now. I would highly recommend that you not move around by yourself for the next few days. At least until you've sold the book or taken it out of this area."

On the way over to the bank, I made a call to Walt's cell phone but he didn't pick up. I wondered whether he had talked to Jen and how that all stood. Dealing with the Great Omar had been taking up all of my energy but I was worried about them. I really hoped they were going to get through it. I liked them both a lot, and I liked them as a couple. They felt like family to me and I think in my mind they represented some stability in a world that over the past year had come unraveled. They were pretty much the last connection I had to my past and if they didn't make it, I was going to be cut off from it completely. So I had selfish reasons for wanting them to make it, but I wanted it for them and for their kids too. I knew that even if they managed to stay together, it was never going to be the same for them. Sometimes things like that make you stronger. Most of the time it seems to go the other way. It seemed to me they both wanted it to work out, especially for the kids.

I was starting to really get a feel for what Megan had been going through. Most of us are so insulated from the things that go on in the world every day. The things we read about in the newspaper. We only really think about it when it strikes close to home. Megan had been immersed in it almost her whole life. The more I understood what she had been going through, the more I admired her. Owning the Great Omar was a moral dilemma for her. It was almost as if she had taken responsibility for all the chaos the book had caused. As if it was up to her to end it once and for all. When we got to the bank, she refused to even touch the box the book was in. I went with her to lock it away. She was genuinely relieved to be rid of it.

"Maybe we should leave it in the bank and just keep driving until we're a thousand miles away."

"Is that really what you want to do, Megan?"

"I don't know what I want to do. I don't want anyone else to die over this thing. Especially somebody who isn't already evil. Especially somebody I care about."

"It'll all be over soon. In time I'm sure you'll remember all of this as some amazing adventure. One of those life changing events that always seem to happen to someone else

"Yeah, well life changing doesn't necessarily mean anything good is going to come from it. Did you ever hear about those people who win the lottery and the next day they go out and get run over by a bus? Somebody up there has a sick sense of humor. It's like we're all playing this cosmic Monopoly game. You're just rolling the dice and going around the board, buying property and stuff until you land on thc Chance square. You pull your card from the deck and it says 'sink hole opens up under your house and everything you own goes down the drain. Glub, glub, glub. Sucks to be you! Do not pass Go'!"

"Sure." I said, laughing. "But that's because they only report the bad news. Nobody wants to read about somebody who got rich overnight and is now living happily ever after."

"I guess. But did you ever wonder what that guy is thinking just before the bus smacks him in the head? He's got to be thinking 'what the hell is this all about'? I mean if you were going to punch my ticket anyway why get me all enthused first. Great, I'm going to be able to afford a gonzo funeral but I'll be dead and nobody wants to go to a funeral anyway, no matter how big a deal they make out of it. At least if I had kicked it before I hit the number I would die knowing that I had reached the end of this stupid meaningless existence and maybe I get to play again. Get a shot at something that doesn't suck so much. What if that kept happening over and over, like that movie 'Groundhog Day'. You keep winning the lottery and every time you eat it in some new and interesting way. How bad would that suck?"

"Well, maybe you get it right eventually."

"Maybe, but if I suddenly bite it after this is all over you need to promise to tie a note to my big toe that says, 'if you hear the word Omar, run away!'"

"I promise. Anyway what do you want to do about dinner tonight?"

"Well the detective thinks we should be staying home, so why don't we order a pizza. We could take the beds apart and make a big fort and we could hide in there and tell scary stories."

"Would that make you feel better?"

"Probably not. But at least I could laugh at you."

"You do that anyway."

"Yeah, but it would give me something to blackmail you with later on."

"Okay. We can order a pizza but I think we better stick to renting a movie."

24

We awoke on Saturday morning to overcast skies and a light drizzle. The ocean was gray and restless under a blanket of thick fog and there was a damp, chilly breeze coming in off the water. The sound of the waves was muted, as if they were breaking far out to sea. The news about Wesley's murder and the suspicion that Badra was likely still in pursuit of the book made me uneasy. My inclination was to stay close to home, but it wasn't the kind of day to hang around a beach-front condo. After breakfast we drove over to the Town Center Mall. Megan did a little window shopping but most of the time we just walked around talking about everything under the sun. She told me about the time she had found a new-born baby in a dumpster and the strange circumstances that had led her to it. A stranger she met on the subway asked Megan to deliver a letter for her. I couldn't imagine anyone else in the world agreeing to do that. But that was Megan. On the way back, she heard the baby crying and she took her to the hospital. Saved the baby's life without giving it a second thought. For anyone else it would have been the dramatic event of a lifetime. For Megan, it was just something else that happened that day. I believed the stories she told me. I knew she wasn't making them up, but I thought for the most part she was making connections that existed only in her own mind. Finding significance in what were actually just random occurrences and jumping to conclusions without knowing all the facts. I had to admit, though, an unusual number of strange events had happened in her life. What I didn't know then, was that I was about to find myself in the middle of one of them.

We decided to pass on the food court and go somewhere nicer for lunch. The rain had stopped but it was still overcast and cool. On the way out to the car, my phone rang.

"Listen to me carefully." the voice said. "We have your friend Mr. Biers. He has not been harmed but if you do not do as I say, you will never see him again. Now you will put the young woman on the phone."

"Whatever you want to say to her you can say to me."

"Do not trifle with me, Mr. Macmillan. Do not doubt that I will do as I say. Now put the young woman on the phone."

Before I could say anything else, Megan took the phone out of my hand.

"Who is this?"

"How do I know you haven't hurt him? I want to talk to him."

There was a pause.

"Ham? Is that you?" Are you okay?"

"No. I can't do that. I don't give a damn about the book. It's not worth your life or anybody else's. How did they ... Ham?"

There was another pause.

"All right I'll do it. Just don't hurt him or I'll throw the damned thing in the ocean. I swear I will. Don't you dare lay a finger on him."

"All right, but it has to be a public place. Someplace where there are people around."

She listened for another few seconds and then hung up the phone.

"They want the book. They want us to go get it now at the bank and take it to the airport. He said we should call Ham's number when we get close and he would give us further directions."

"I'm going to call Benjamin."

"No. Please don't do that, Mark. I couldn't stand it if Ham got hurt over this thing. They can have the damned book. I don't care anymore."

"How do we know they won't kill him anyway? And us too for that matter."

"It'll be a public place. I told him I wouldn't do it otherwise. It'll be okay. Why would they risk hurting anybody at a public place if they didn't have to? Let's just go to the bank and get it."

"Do you think it was Badra?"

"I don't know. You heard him, he has an accent. It could have been that Alfarsi guy. I'm so sick of this. I swear if they didn't have Ham I would throw the damned thing off a cliff. They know we put it in the bank. How could they know that? They must have been following us. They must know everything."

On the way over to the bank my mind was racing. At that point I wasn't worried about losing the book either, but I was afraid Megan was going to get hurt. I kept checking the rear view mirror to see if there was anyone following us. I didn't know what to do. When we arrived at the bank I managed to find a parking spot across from the entrance. We sat for a moment in silence.

"Are you sure this is what you want to do, Megan? I don't think they're really going to hurt him. We could call Benjamin and have the airport searched."

"No. I don't want to risk it. I'm just going to do what he asked."

"Well then after we get the book, I'm going to take you back to the condo. I'll meet them by myself."

She looked over at me then with an expression I hadn't seen before.

"I don't want to seem ungrateful, Mark, but this is my life. I know you're trying to protect me and I love that about you but I have to do this. I think somehow this is part of my destiny. I think maybe my whole life has been about this moment. I can't hide from it. I can't let somebody else do it for me. Do you understand?"

"Not really. But if that's what you want, I'm not going to get in the way. But I am coming with you. You're not going to talk me out of that."

She leaned over and kissed me then.

"Okay. Let's get it over with."

As we started to get out of the car someone came up behind Megan and pushed her back onto the seat. I couldn't see who it was until he reached in and put a knife to her throat. It was Badra. I started to react until I realized he wasn't going to do anything, at least until he had the book. He removed a cable tie from his pocket and handed it to me.

"If you don't do as I say I'll kill her. Now strap your left wrist to the steering wheel. Make sure it's tight."

I did what I was told. He took another tie and gave it to Megan. Now strap his right wrist to the wheel. Megan looked at me. There was sadness and resignation on her face, but she didn't look afraid. I sat there in stunned silence. I had never been confined before and the rage was starting to bubble up inside of me. I forced myself to calm down. He was in control now and the look on his face turned to a malicious smirk. He pulled Megan out roughly by her arm.

"You know what I want. I have someone in the bank to watch you so don't raise an alarm or make any calls. You understand?"

Megan nodded.

"Now give me your phone."

"I don't have one."

"What kind of bitch doesn't have a phone?"

He reached down and patted her pockets and then let go of her arm.

"I'm going to stay here with your boyfriend. If you do anything stupid I'm going to kill him. You understand?"

Megan nodded again. Badra got into the passenger seat. He watched her walk across the street and up the walkway into the bank. Once she was inside he turned to me.

"So what are you some kind of a stupid hick cop or something? Did you think I didn't notice you and the little bitch watching me in the car the other day? Why did you think I opened the case right in front of you on the street. I was going to wave the book right under your fucking nose. To show you what a fool you are."

"Yeah. Well how did that work out for you?"

He reached over and pushed the point of his knife into the back of my hand until it started to bleed. He twisted the blade until I grimaced in pain. He smiled at me.

"We'll see who has the last laugh. When I get the book I'm going to kill you first. Then I'm going to take the little bitch somewhere quiet and I'm going to bleed her. I'm going to enjoy listening to her scream."

I knew I had to do something before it was too late. I didn't really believe he was going to harm us. Once he got the book it would serve no purpose other than the enjoyment he would get from it. It would only put him more at risk. He certainly wasn't going to do anything where there could be witnesses. He was either going to run, or he was going to make me drive somewhere. To do that he would have to free my hands and that's when I would hit him. Megan was not helpless. She was strong and she knew how to handle herself. I knew she wouldn't panic. She would not let him cut her without a fight. I just needed her to hold him off for a second until I could get in close. I hoped it wouldn't come to that, but there was no way I was going to let him be alone with her. We waited in silence. It seemed like a very long time had passed and Badra was starting to get nervous.

"She better not be fucking with me. She better get her ass out here now or I'm going in after her."

Just then I saw the door open. Megan stepped out of the bank, but she wasn't alone. I didn't understand what was going on. There was a man with her. I didn't recognize him. He was middle aged with thinning blond hair and the beginnings of a pot belly hanging over his belt. At first I thought it must have been the guy Badra said would be watching her in the bank but it was obvious Badra didn't know who it was either. They stopped for a moment in front of the door and it looked like they were having a casual conversation. In a moment the guy reached over and put his hand on Megan's shoulder. She smiled at him. Then she held out the cardboard box as if she were going to give it to him. Badra went berserk. He punched the dashboard and started cursing.

"Who the fuck is that?"

"I never saw him before." I said.

"Did she think I was making a joke? I'm going to cut her fucking head off."

He leapt out of the car, slamming the door behind him, and then he ran across the street. He never saw the truck coming. There was the shrill scream of tires skidding on pavement and the smell of burnt rubber, followed by a sickening thud. Badra's body landed awkwardly, thirty feet down the road. His head was twisted in a way that left no doubt that he was dead. The force of the blow had knocked him right out of his shoes which were sitting side by side on the road as if he had taken them off to go to bed.

I sat there stunned, just staring at his lifeless body lying in the street, and then I looked over at Megan. She was standing alone in front of the bank holding the cardboard box. The man she had been talking to was gone. I think I must have gone into shock. My mind couldn't make any sense of it. The truck driver hesitated for a moment and then he stepped on the gas and tore off down the road, nearly running over Badra a second time. A woman screamed and a crowd began to gather. Some people were bent over the body, trying to help him. Everyone's attention

343

was on Badra now except for a few men who were running after the truck, trying to get the license number. Megan walked calmly over to the car and got in. She looked over at me. There was a look of concern on her face.

"Are you okay?" She asked in a calm, level voice.

I just nodded.

"I think we'd better get out of here, don't you?"

I asked her to open the console and get the penknife I kept there for emergencies. She managed to cut through the cable ties and she insisted on taking a tissue and some hand cleaner to the cut on my hand.

"Do you have a first aid kit?"

"I think there's one in the glove box."

She removed the kit and took out a Band-Aid. She placed it over the wound. It was as if nothing at all had happened and she had all the time in the world. I started the car and drove away slowly, watching my rear view mirror to see if anyone had noticed us. It appeared no one had seen Badra get out of my car before he was hit. There was no time to worry about it.

"What the hell just happened, Megan? Who was that guy you were talking to?"

"I don't know." She said, smiling. "I never saw him before."

There was something very different about her. She seemed somehow detached and amazingly calm. Almost serene. I was so hyped up I was starting to shake and I was having difficulty concentrating on my driving. I didn't know what to say so I said nothing.

"I need to use your phone." She said, after a few moments of silence.

"What are you going to do?"

"I'm going to call Ham's phone and talk to whoever is holding him. Badra's dead so it has to be Alfarsi. I'm going to make him a deal for the book."

There was no doubt in my mind that Megan had taken complete control of the situation and had worked out exactly what she was going to do. I was too spent to even question her about it. From then on it was going to be her show and I was just along for the ride. It was as if our roles had been completely reversed and I was the one adrift in some strange new world.

Megan made the call. They were not at Miami International airport. Alfarsi was with Ham at the Kendall-Tamiami Executive Airport a few miles to the southwest. He told Megan to meet him at the Air Sal terminal. Megan insisted that he be alone except for Ham. We drove down to Miami in silence. I didn't know what to say to her and she also seemed at a loss for words. I found the airport pretty easily, but it took me a little while to locate the right building. The terminal lounge was small and we had no trouble finding them. Ham was sitting next to an older man with olive skin and neatly cut gray hair. He was wearing an expensive suit and smoking a long, thin cigarette. Ham looked dejected but he brightened up when we entered. Megan walked over and sat down across from them. She looked over at Ham.

"Are you okay Ham. Did they hurt you?"

"No. I haven't been harmed. Are you all right?"

"Yeah, I'm fine. We're both fine."

She turned to Alfarsi.

"Your friend is dead."

"I'm sorry. Who is dead?"

"You know who I'm talking about. Badra. The bastard you sent to kill us."

"I sent no one to do any such thing. I don't know what you're talking about. I am simply here to negotiate the purchase of the Great Omar. Now may we please get down to business? My plane is waiting for me."

"All right. I don't care if you own up to it or not. Here's the deal. I will sell you the Great Omar for four million dollars and I won't negotiate the price. You and I both know it's worth a whole lot more than that but I'm tired of dealing with it. I'm tired of people dying over it. I'm tired of being around assholes like you. We have the book here with us. It's Saturday and my bank closes in one hour. What I need you to do is to have the four million wired directly into my account at this bank."

She handed Alfarsi a deposit slip.

"If you don't agree we're going to walk away with the book. The police know about you, so if you want it, this is going to be your only chance. Once the money shows up in my account I'll give you the Great Omar and you can take it with you wherever you're going, or straight to hell for all I care."

347

We all just stared at her. I was too astounded to say anything. I didn't know how she even knew you could wire money into someone's account. She had only had an account at all for a couple of days. I was holding the box on my lap, ready to bolt out of the building with it if things went wrong. Ham was smiling. He nodded his head at her as if to say, 'well done'. Alfarsi was silent for a moment. He had a strange look on his face. It was a mixture of displeasure at having been backed into a corner along with what looked like grudging respect for this young woman who had put him there. He looked over at the box on my lap.

"There is no reason for unpleasantness. This is merely a negotiation." He pointed to the box. "I assume this is the Great Omar?"

"Yeah, that's it." Megan said. "Do we have a deal?"

"May I see the book please?"

"I opened the box and pulled back the tissue paper. I passed it over to Ham."

"This is indeed The Great Omar." Ham said. "I have examined it thoroughly and I will stake my reputation on it."

Alfarsi stared at the book. He reached down and drew his finger lightly across the cover. He opened the book carefully and examined some of the illustrations. A look came over his face that was almost like lust.

"Very well. We have a deal."

He stood up and walked over to a corner of the lounge and punched a number into his phone. There was a short conversation and then he read the account and routing numbers into the phone and then repeated them. When he was finished, he put the phone in his pocket and walked back over to us. We all sat in silence for what seemed like an eternity. No one was in the mood for making small talk. Aflarsi had a smug look on his face. He was obviously pleased with the way things had turned out. He opened his briefcase and removed some papers.

"This is a bill of sale which I have already prepared. I will enter the agreed upon price and ask you to sign please. I would ask Mr. Biers to stand as witness to our agreement."

Alfarsi signed the document and Ham signed as witness. Megan refused to sign until she got word that the funds were transferred. We all waited again in silence.

"Where are you going to keep it? Ham asked, finally."

"My collection is currently housed at my estate in Croydon, just south of London. I have awaited this moment for a very long time. A place of honor awaits it. By this time tomorrow The Great Omar will be home at last. I have many valuable works of art at my estate but I must tell you, the Omar will be the crown jewel of my collection. If you are ever in London, please get in touch. It would be my pleasure to show you my holdings."

He looked at his watch and then turned to Megan.

"Why don't you try your bank, young lady? The funds should have arrived by now."

I gave Megan my phone. She had a business card with the banks phone number in her checkbook. She called and requested confirmation of the deposit. We were all staring at her while she waited. Finally, she looked over at Alfarsi.

"It's there." She said, with no expression on her face. "The book is yours now and believe me, you deserve it."

Megan signed the papers and Alfarsi gave her a copy. She stood up and looked over at Ham and she smiled for the first time since we arrived at the terminal. "Can we take you someplace?"

Ham looked a little stunned.

"I would appreciate a ride to my hotel, if you wouldn't mind."

Megan turned and walked out of the terminal without looking back. Ham and I followed behind her like a couple of school boys on a class trip. When we were all in the car she looked at us and smiled.

"I chose four million dollars for a reason. I figured there would be some taxes or something and then there are your expenses, Ham. That should leave at least a million for each of us. That was the deal I made with you Ham. A third of the proceeds. I know you probably could have gotten more, but I didn't want that damned book to get into the hands of some honest collector who might get hurt by it and I just want to be rid of it. It's killed too many people already. It killed Badra now too but he deserved it. Maybe most of the people it killed deserved it but I don't have to worry about it any more. It belongs with that evil bastard in there now and I hope it never sees the light of day again."

"I'm more than happy with the outcome, Megan, and profoundly impressed by the way you handled it. Well done!"

"How did they get hold of you, Ham?" I asked.

"Alfarsi said he wanted to make me an offer on the Great Omar. When I declined he told me a very ruthless individual was also in pursuit of the book and was following you. He said the best way to insure your safety was to make a deal with him now, before this other individual got too close."

"So he didn't admit Badra was working for him?"

"No. Alfarsi is a clever man. I would be willing to wager there is no evidence at all connecting the two of them. He would have gotten the book either way. How was Badra killed?"

"He was hit by a truck when he tried to get the book from me."

Ham just shook his head. "That is astounding!"

I looked over at Megan. There was no way I was going to take her money. Before I could say anything though, she smiled and waved her finger at me.

"And I don't want to hear any more from you about how you can't take my money. We've been in this together from jump and that money is yours. I thought about it a long time and I decided a million dollars was just the right number for me anyway. Enough to rearrange my life, but not enough to turn me into a griller. Besides, you already spent about a million dollars on me, so it's payback time. If you really don't want it you can give it away. To anybody except me."

25

Late in the afternoon I got a call from detective Benjamin. He wanted us to know that Badra had been killed in a hit and run accident near where we were staying in Boca Raton. He commented that someone must be looking out for us because Badra most likely had found out were we were staying and was probably watching us. I didn't tell him about our run-in at the bank. There was no point. I just thanked him for letting us know.

That evening we had a light dinner at a beach bar near the condo. The storm had passed and it was another beautiful evening. After dinner, we were watching the sunset and relaxing over some drinks when Megan grabbed my arm.

"Come on. There's one last thing I have to do."

She took a dinner roll from the basket and then led me out onto the beach.

"What are you going to do?"

"Feed the seagulls."

It was one of the things I had come to love about her. The joy and spontaneity that bubbled up suddenly from deep within her. Like a child, and all the more beautiful because she had never let it fade away. I watched her as she tore off small pieces of bread and cast them up into the sky for the seagulls to catch. In seconds there was an entire flock of them screaming above our heads. Megan reached into her pocket and pulled out a small plastic envelope. She emptied it into the palm of her hand. It was the small ruby that had come loose from the Great Omar. She put a piece of bread in her mouth to moisten it and then she took the stone and pushed it into the center. She bent her knees and flung the bread as high as she could. One of the seagulls caught it and then wheeled out to sea. She looked at me and smiled.

"Now it's over."

We stayed out on the beach long after sunset. Megan seemed entirely at peace with herself. I was relieved that everything had worked out in the end but I was still coming to grips with how close it had come to ending badly. I was a little angry with myself for letting Badra get

355

control of me without putting up a fight. I knew it was better that it worked out as it had, but that didn't help. I was beginning to change my mind about Megan's view of reality. I was starting to believe there really were other forces at work in the world. Things we couldn't see or understand. It was still hard for me to accept that there was any such thing as a cursed object, but if there were, The Great Omar was surely one of them. I couldn't even count the number of people who had lost their lives after getting involved with it. Somehow Megan had avoided the fate of so many others who had owned the book. Maybe it was because among them all, she was the only one who didn't really want it. Refused even to touch it. She was perhaps the only person since its creation who refused to compromise her values and beliefs for the promise of great wealth. In the end, she knew it really was just a book of poetry. Poetry that celebrates life in the here and now, and tells us to enjoy it while we can.

I knew also that our adventure was coming to an end and I was down about it. In spite of the danger and the chaos, spending time with Megan was one of the best things that had ever happened to me. I think Rachel was right. It had been at least as much about Megan helping me. I was going to miss having her with me every day, but we couldn't stay on vacation forever.

Both of us had to make new lives for ourselves. I think Megan was feeling it too and hanging over it all was that question about us. Whether we'd be able to find a way to stay in each others lives. We made love that night, slowly and tenderly. Alive in that moment with no thought of the future or the past and no regrets. Just two lonely people who had been thrown together by the unfathomable mechanism of a clockwork universe. Pieces in some grand cosmic design that no human being is given to understand. When I fell asleep that night, it felt like we had finally put it all behind us. I thought we had finally seen the last of the strange events that had surrounded the Great Omar since its creation. But the book had not yet lost its ability to astonish or to permanently rearrange my understanding of the world. I was awakened in the morning by my phone ringing. It was Ham. He sounded a little excited and he asked if we had been watching the news. I put the phone down and flipped on CNN. Megan slid over behind me and rested her chin on my shoulder. She put her arms around my waist.

"What's going on?"

"I don't know. Ham said we should put on the news. He didn't say why. He just said to call him later."

... Overnight a tornado touched down near the small town of Woodward Oklahoma. It is in a rural area of the state and the damage was limited to just a few houses, a barn and a grain silo. There were, however, six killed and at least twenty nine injured. Rescue teams are still combing through the debris in case there are more victims buried under the rubble.

In other news, a small private jet has gone missing over the North Atlantic. The flight originated in Miami Florida and made a refueling stop at JFK in New York City. It was on route to London's Gatwick airport when the pilot reported he had lost an engine and was going to divert to Gander, Newfoundland International airport. The plane never reached that destination. The jet was a Gulfstream V and was owned by billionaire art collector Daoud Ali Alfarsi who is believed to have been on board. We do not yet know if there were other passengers on the flight. Typically the crew would consist of two pilots and a cabin attendant. We have aviation expert Thomas Jorgensen on the phone with us.

Mr. Jorgensen, thank you for your time. Do we have any additional information about this incident?

Yes. We have been told that there was a second radio transmission one minute and forty six seconds after the original distress call. The pilot reported having difficulty with his second engine and he radioed his position. Shortly after that transmission the plane disappeared from radar.

What would cause an aircraft to lose both of its engines like that?

I can't answer that question with any certainty. There have been cases in the past where contaminated fuel was involved but there could have been a number of different causes. We may find out if we're able to recover the black boxes, but for now it would just be speculation.

Has there been any sighting of wreckage or perhaps a life raft in the area?

Nothing has been reported but they lost contact with the aircraft at just past midnight and could not begin the search until this morning. Search aircraft out of Gander were dispatched at dawn.

Were there any other ships in the area that could lend assistance?

Yes, there was a British cruise ship, MS Balmoral in the area at the time of the distress call. Ironically, it would not normally have been in this part of the Atlantic at this time of year, but it had recently sailed from Southampton, England on a voyage to commemorate the sinking of the Titanic. That terrible tragedy occurred exactly one hundred years ago today near the position radioed by the pilot of the lost aircraft. The captain reported passengers had heard the sound of a plane flying low in the area and that it didn't sound normal. Some reported what sounded like a small explosion, but visibility was very bad at the time and there were no sightings of any flash or fire. We should have more information once the search crews begin reporting in.

We just sat there in stunned silence. Finally Megan turned to me and kissed me on the cheek.

"Alfarsi was right after all. It finally found its way home."

26

Megan departed two days later on a flight to New York. She had never flown before and she was nervous about it. She wanted me to come with her but I had my car and I needed to drive back up to Durham to check on Walt and Jennifer. I hadn't heard any more from Walt and I was a little afraid to call Jen, not knowing if he had come clean with her. It was something I needed to do in person and in the end Megan understood. I promised I would drive up to the city as soon as I could. I made her buy a cell phone so I could get in touch with her. She hated it.

Ham agreed to accompany her on the flight and on her visit to Annabel's lawyer. He was on his way to St. Petersburg where he believed he had uncovered a lead on one of the lost Faberge Golden Eggs. He suggested we could all meet in New York at some point and celebrate our partnership over dinner. We all agreed.

While we were waiting for their flight, Ham took me aside.

"Have you decided what you want to do with your future yet, Mark?"

"No. I have a few options I'm considering but nothing definite."

"Well, I don't know if this is something you would be interested in but perhaps while you are waiting for the right opportunity to come along. I spend a good deal of time in Europe these days and I am in need of someone here in the States who can run down leads for me. It is expensive and very time consuming, not to mention exhausting, to continuously fly back and forth. You would be making contact with individuals who may have information of interest. As you have recently discovered, such inquiries can lead to some very interesting moments. It's fairly addicting actually which is why, I suppose, I have never considered retirement. I don't need someone with police experience per se. Just someone with intelligence and a high degree of integrity. Someone with good instincts. I have come to recognize those qualities in you and I would very much like to continue our association. It would be on a project basis and I would handle all expenses of course. We could negotiate your fee on a case by case basis and if we succeed in digging up any more buried treasure you would be in for a percentage. It wouldn't be full time, of course, but it could be quite lucrative for you and also leave you time to pursue other interests. I don't need an answer right away, but please give it some thought. You have my number."

Before they passed through security, Megan threw her arms around me and squeezed me so hard it was difficult to breathe.

"Don't you leave me all alone to figure this out by myself. You need to get up there as soon as you can. Promise?"

"It should only be two or three days. Call me and let me know how it's going."

"I will, but don't expect any long conversations. I don't like to talk to people unless I can see their face. Especially your face."

The drive up to Durham was long and I felt uneasy. On the way down I had been really looking forward to seeing Walt and Jen. Now I was dreading it. I felt sorry for both of them but mostly for Jennifer. I was still angry with Walt for letting himself fall so far, but he was my friend and the last thing he needed was for me to turn my back on him now. I had tried several times to reach him by phone with no success. Reluctantly I called Jen, not knowing if Walt had told her everything or not. She didn't sound too happy to hear from me but she asked me to come by. I didn't know what to expect when I knocked on the door but she gave me a hug and invited me in. The kids were at school.

"Thank you for coming, Mark. I'm really sorry you had to get involved with all of this. Walt told me you gave him a loan. You really are a good friend."

"I'm glad I could help."

"I was mad at you for a while for not being completely honest with me, but I know we put you in the middle and that wasn't fair."

"I wanted to tell you what was going on, Jen, but Walt needed to do that himself."

"I know. I'm sorry."

"So where is he? I haven't been able to reach him on the phone."

"He flew out to California. There's a company out there that's interested in his program. He said it looks pretty good. I guess he didn't want to talk to you until it's settled one way or another. That, and he really is ashamed. I think it was almost as hard to tell you as it was to tell me."

"How are you dealing with it?"

"I guess I'm really still in shock. To tell you the truth, I'm not sure how I feel. I still care about him, even after everything, but I don't know if I'm ever going to be able to trust him again. I'm really afraid about the drugs. I've been doing a lot of reading about it and so many people relapse. He still doesn't seem right to me. The kids are happy he's back, but I'm almost afraid for them to be alone with him. I know that's wrong. It's going to take some time. I keep going back and forth between feeling sorry for him and being angry with him. I don't seem to have any control of it. You know what the worst part is? I don't feel proud of him anymore. Before, when we were out together I always felt this confidence about us. About our lives. I don't feel that any more. It feels like people know, even though I'm mostly sure they don't. I'm almost afraid to look our friends in the eye anymore. That's the part I hate the most. It's the part that makes me the most angry."

"He'll make you proud again. He's lucky to have you and he knows it. A lot of women would have just walked away."

"Don't think I didn't consider it. At first I didn't even want him in the house, but I couldn't do that to the kids. I'm struggling with it. I'm trying to hold on. I don't know if we're going to make it. I mean he gambled away our life savings without even asking me. How could he do something like that, let alone the drugs? I'm having a hard time believing he cares about me at all. Honestly, if it weren't for the kids I would have left him already."

"I think you need to give it a little time, Jen. It's all too raw now and it's not a good time to make any big decisions. Maybe this will be a good thing for your marriage in the long run. Maybe Walt will end up being better for it. Appreciate you more."

"We'll see. Right now I can't imagine even getting past this."

"Are you okay financially. If you need help, don't be afraid to ask."

"We'll be okay but we're going to have to downsize a little. Walt's company has been shuttered since Charley passed away, so a lot will depend on where he finds work. The job market down here isn't the greatest right now but I'm sure he'll find something. It could mean relocating. We may have to move anyway. This whole mess has pretty much wiped out our safety net. That's happened to a lot of people in the last few years though, through no fault of their own. I'm determined not to feel sorry for myself. I'm actually going back to work. I've been offered a position in the Fine Arts department at the University. It's only part time for now, but it'll be good for me. I'll still be here when the kids get home from school and it will help me get my mind off of everything. It's what I need right now."

"I think you're right. Look, I meant it about the money. If you need help just pick up the phone. I know Walt wouldn't want to ask me again but you can. I don't want to keep anything from him but you can always ask me. I don't want this to be any harder for you than it already is. Tell Walt if he needs another loan before he can close a deal, I can do that."

She reached up and kissed me then. It was a warm and lingering kiss and I could feel the emotion and the conflict in her body. She broke away from me suddenly and stepped back. She looked up at me.

"I'm just so confused about everything."

"I know."

"Hey, I've been so busy unloading my problems I didn't even ask about you. What's been going on? What ever became of Megan?"

I didn't know where to begin. We went into the kitchen and she poured us some coffee. I spent the next hour telling her about the Great Omar and everything that had happened since I had last seen her. She was astounded and it showed on her face. When I had finished she was silent for a moment, then she shook her head.

"That's incredible. I can't believe all of that happened since I saw you last. What has it been? Four or five weeks? It doesn't even seem possible."

"I know. I still wake up sometimes and think it was all a dream."

"So what's going to happen now? Are you and Megan going to get together? Are you going to move to New York?"

"I have no idea. I'm heading back up to the city when I leave here and I plan to spend some time with her. Then we'll see. I'm in no hurry and she isn't either."

"Are you going to take your friend Ham up on his offer? It sounds exciting? So different from what you've been doing up to now."

"Well, different is what I'm going for these days."

"I'll say!"

"I think I might give it a try. I don't know how interesting it actually will be. I think it'll mostly be pretty routine but at least I'll be doing something that'll engage my brain and I'll be able to travel a little. Ask me in a year. I'll be able to give you a better answer then."

"I'll do that. Please stay in touch, Mark. You know there's always going to be a place in my heart for you."

I had a lot of time to think on the drive back up to New York. It was a little easier to be objective about my life without having Megan there next to me. If nothing else, it made me realize how much I missed her. The car felt cold inside and turning up the heater didn't help. I think talking to Jen about Megan had helped me understand it all a little better. The one thing I didn't mention was the man who had showed up outside of the bank on the day Badra was killed. I didn't mention it because I still don't understand it myself. It seemed to me Megan had somehow tapped into a kind of elemental force in the world. Not in the sense of having some kind of power. In fact it was really the exact opposite of that. Her strength came from accepting her life fully, and focusing on everyone around her instead of getting lost in herself. She did what she thought was right and let everything else take care of itself. And when living that way got her into trouble, she believed in her heart that someone would come along and get in the way.

Epilogue

When Megan visited Annabel's lawyer for the reading of her Will she was hoping perhaps she could take a few keepsakes from the apartment to remember her by. She got a lot more than that. Even though Annabel didn't have much in the way of savings, she owned the building she lived in and also the property in North Williamsburg that had once held her father's bookstore. She gave it all to Megan. It took her a while to get over the shock. She called me right after and she was babbling so much it was hard to understand what she was saying. In the end she just shouted that she had a house to live in. A house in New York. She asked me again to come see her as soon as I could.

Megan moved into the empty apartment across the hall from the one Annabel had lived in. She kept Annabel's apartment vacant and unchanged. It became a place where her friends could take shelter for a little while if they didn't have anywhere else to stay. The book shop property had been vacant for nearly a year, having last housed a boutique. Megan immediately got to work converting the space into a gallery. I spent nearly a month being her handyman and jack of all trades. The transformation I saw in her was remarkable. She named the gallery the Annabel Weiss Art Cooperative. It's a place where struggling artists can hang their work on a consignment basis, with Megan taking a small percentage when they sell. It has become one of those places tourists like to discover when they wander over to Brooklyn, and where high end galleries come to see what's trending. The third floor loft was also opened up and turned into a studio. Megan tells me the light is really good in the morning. It's a place where budding artists can work for free as long as they follow the rules. These are posted on the door, just below a small acrylic painting entitled 'Dog Crap with Gum Wrapper'. No Drugs, No Alcohol, and No Bullshit. The latter being loosely defined as anything that pisses Megan off. She also made a substantial donation to a local soup kitchen and she eats there herself from time to time to make sure the food is up to her standards. She made me try it and it really was pretty good.

We get together whenever I'm in the City, which is a lot these days. We have dinner at a nice restaurant and I stay over at her place. Sometimes we make love. We stay up late talking about life and destiny and about Megan's world. That fascinating and magical place at the bottom of the rabbit hole that in the end, even a million dollars couldn't change. Now and then Megan takes me on guided tours of her favorite places in the city and she introduces me to her street friends. I've spent a few very entertaining evenings having conversations around a campfire under a bridge. There really are some interesting people out there in the world. I've asked Megan many times if she's ever going to get a boyfriend and her pat answers is. 'You'll have to do. I don't have the time to break anyone else in'. Megan started taking art classes again and her paintings are really very good. Her unique relationship with the world comes through in a way that's unmistakable but difficult to describe. She picked out one she thought Jen would like and she sent it down to her. She still draws her caricatures in the park sometimes if the weather's nice. If you're ever up by the Guggenheim look for her across the street. She'll be the beautiful young woman with sapphire blue eyes and red hair, like an ember. You'll know it's her by the gold necklace she always wears. It's a little girl on a bicycle with a round hat and ribbons hanging down the back. If she likes you, she might even show you the inscription on the back.

Also by Wallace F. Brown:

The Shepherd Sleeps

Jayapura

The Echo Stones